House

House

by

Pauline Holdstock

A Porcépic Book
Beach Holme Publishers
Victoria, B.C.

Special thanks and love to Sue, and to Ant, and to Jack for the bricks and the mortar.

Copyright © 1994 by Pauline Holdstock

First Canadian Edition

This edition published by
Beach Holme Publishers
4252 Commerce Circle, Victoria, B.C. V8Z 4M2
with thanks to The Canada Council
and the B.C. Ministry of Tourism and Culture
for their assistance.
This is a Porcépic Book.

Thank you to Hamish Hamilton, Penguin Books Ltd. (UK) (London, England) for permission to use the lines from "Two Invocations Of Death" © Kathleen Raine, 1956, from *Kathleen Rain's Collected Poems.*

Cover Art: Sue Hemingway
Cover Design: Antonia Banyard and Barbara Munzar
Production Editors: Antonia Banyard, Jessie Carrick
Thank you to Piper Giles for the use of her foot.

Canadian Cataloguing in Publication Data

    Holdstock, Pauline,
      House

    "A Porcépic Book"
    ISBN 0-88878-353-1
    I. Title.
    PS8565.O622H6 1994   C813'.54   C94-910321-7
    PR9199.3.H64H6 1994

for John

Other Books by Pauline Holdstock

The Blackbird's Song (novel)

The Burial Ground (novel)

Swimming From the Flames (forthcoming, short stories)

Contents

From a place I came
That was never in time,
From the beat of a heart
that was never in pain.

From "Two Invocations Of Death,"
Kathleen Raine

The Kitchen

"Shove over." Obediently Tots shifted her chair to make room for Scoria.

With the others, Haggerty, Mildred, Mrs. Phelum, and the two parlour maids, Morgan-The-Not-Very-Fey and Sherilee, there were seven in all. But Mrs. Phelum never counted, or if she did it was only to cut the pie.

Come one, come all. The kitchen door, down the steps beneath the front door, stood open winter and summer admitting horseflies and passing vagrants. Mrs. Phelum did not object to either. At the first sign of a visitor she would fling open her store of jolly clichés.

She was all bounty. She was Nell Gwyn with a full bushel. Even to wandering evangelists and the estate agents who visited regularly, Mrs. Phelum was geniality itself. It is possible that she was clinically, chronically happy, gripped from within by a terminal contentment, for there was nothing evident about her place, her position that is, except of course the food, that might be expected to bring on such good humour. Nothing certainly about the House.

The House, a large square pile of stuccoed brick several storeys high—you might be drawn to say 'tall'—was in an advanced state of dilapidation. All along Croxleigh Place roofs sagged and walls bowed; chimney pots and drain pipes lay in the dusty gardens behind. London was full of vacant premises that no one could afford to keep; the dispossessed now possessed the streets. Most of the buildings were boarded and nailed against squatters and stood empty except for the echo of guard dogs left behind to bark outrageously at their misfortune. The façades, which had once shone in the sun, were strictly symmetrical, except where they had slipped out of true, but their smooth white icing was flaking now and had fallen away in places, revealing the brick. All of the houses were topped with chunks of the dangerous stuff at the parapet and all sported red burglar alarms like poppies from their days of glory. The front door of the House, like those of its neighbours, was solid and central, fortified within by locks and bolts, top, bottom, and middle, and properly elevated above the plebian street to which stone steps descended. Below street level, on either side of the steps, grimy windows looked out into deep areas surrounded by black iron railings, lumpy now with rust. Before the Mishap, the House might have commanded almost any price on the market. A person could smell the money in Belgravia from one of the upper windows. In theory the Master had only to sell it in order to move wherever he wished; in practice he had swallowed up his buyers. The House had become his personal albatross. It was large, it kept the occupants reasonably dry, but it rarely kept them warm. It was draughty and dirty, dilapidated and decaying, suffered from wet rot as well as dry and played accommodating host to the death watch beetle. Mrs. Phelum nevertheless continued to bloom and beam amid the less than perfect appointments of her workplace—appointments listed variously as 'rare', 'fine', and 'unique' by the sharp-shouldered salesmen.

She had her girls of course to help her, and Haggerty.

The table at which they sat this morning for elevenses was a great long, wide, cracked and sway-backed thing. But it could seat twelve. An eel pie rested on it like a pale scab. Mrs. Phelum tried not to pay too much attention to the pie. It was about time it was eaten. But just let anyone try to say it was past it.

"You cut it, Mildred," said Mrs. Phelum. And while Mildred made feeble inroads into the pie and delivered disintegrating, undersized portions all round, the cook occupied herself with a calendar.

"Now then." She had to tear off several pages of vapid-eyed pets sitting in unlikely places before she reached August. Normally she relied on the printout that stuttered daily from the ancient computer in the still-room—huge outmoded presence it was—to tell her the date, but this morning Ben had found the calendar and had at once recognized that although it was forty-five years out of date its days coincided with those of the current year.

"Ah. Here we are." August was the month in which the Master's birthday fell occasioning the annual Day Out—August 6—for all members of the Household. It took some organizing.

"August—thanks ducks, I'll have a bigger bit—the sixth. Day after tomorrow. Don't know where the days go." She took a bite of pie and began marking off a row of callous crosses. "Nor the years. Oh, well. Can't be helped. You're as young as you feel. Can't live forever...."

"How old are you, then?" Scoria cut in.

Sherilee removed a piece of eel from her mouth with her fork—she took a long time to chew—and said, "That's not a question to ask in polite company."

Mildred only looked alarmed. Mildred, it is just possible, had early been frightened into subjection and fervent loyalty by Mrs. Phelum's enormous breasts. She was in any event most timid and withdrawn and prone to nervous disorders of every kind. She made her presence felt in her own way, however; could indicate, for instance, simply by the manner of her walking that her tooth was playing up; could telegraph merely by holding her teacup at a certain angle that she had one of her heads; and there was no mistaking when it was her 'time', which seemed to be most of the time.

"As old as me tongue and older than me teeth," answered Mrs. Phelum.

"Well I'm forty and in fine fettle, thank you very much," said Morgan, who was. The word mettlesome might have been coined for

Morgan. Six foot one in her high heels, she carried herself about the house with long, swinging strides, purposeful and efficient, no less imposing for the ribboned cap she wore, and no less vigorous for the fact that she smoked and drank with serious intent. The cap, along with her black, seamed stockings, was part of the uniform the Master insisted on for her and for Sherilee. Every morning the two maids put on their little black dresses and frilly aprons and fixed their caps. Sherilee, with the brown hair and brown eyes of a puppy and the discernment and strength of mind to match, looked suitably biddable. Morgan, androgynous and mildly threatening, looked like someone you might have met in the Bois de Boulogne at two in the morning.

She had inherited her Scots accent, along with her black hair and a strong taste for crime, from her mother who had suffered from a pathological need to fill her pockets (and Morgan's too at times) before she left a building. Time and again she had spent little 'breaks' away. Morgan, an observant child, never forgot the thrill induced by the moment of crime but she kept a mental file of notes on certain mistakes she would not make when she grew up. The predilection may have been learned but the accent was stamped on her soul, a brand, a genetic imprint it might have been, like the possession of two legs. Morgan liked to preen her accent in public. It was intimidating.

Sherilee looked at her fondly. She was so strong. Sherilee herself would only confess, with a coy glance at Haggerty, to being over twenty-one.

But Haggerty was not taking notice. He lapped at his tea.

Mildred's dreadful secret, which everyone knew, began to work at the back of her throat, and would come out.

"I'm not in any hurry to reach twenty-one," she began and went on to tell not for the first time how a fortune-teller had read her tea-leaves and predicted sudden death. It was slated for her twenty-first birthday and she had been drinking several cups of tea a day ever since in an effort to avert it; but the readings were invariably dismal and supported Scoria's opinion that when the day came there would be found not a drop of blood in Mildred's veins, but plenty of weak tea.

"That was when you wouldn't pay up wasn't it? You shouldn't never cross a gypsy's path—"

"Black cat's," corrected Morgan. She tipped back her head and exhaled a fast jet of cigarette smoke.

"That's right. It's bad luck." Sherilee's general knowledge was wobbly but she was certain of some things.

"—without crossing her palm with silver," finished Mrs. Phelum, pleased to have got it straight, if only in her own mind.

Haggerty belched. "Thanks for the tea, mum," he said and left. Haggerty was as much a fixture in the Household as Mrs. Phelum. No one really knew whether he was in fact her son. He was simply there, outside in the dust.

He was indispensible. He grew the vegetables and he supplied the range. His potatoes and his onions sprouted from a row of galvanised wash tubs at the bottom of the garden. In case of foragers, he locked up the tubs each night along with the chickens in the shed where he slept. By day he constructed wood piles from the lumber of derelict buildings, which were in plentiful supply. Whole doors and staircases he sawed and chopped to equal lengths for Mrs. Phelum's stove. It consumed the time.

Occasionally he used the wood to build, repairing the House when the woodworm had been busy, something that was only evident when doors fell from frames and entire windows dropped out of walls. He would carve out the damaged sections, bit by bit replacing them with salvage, from which he had carved out the damaged sections ....

Once his tedious labour had taken a brief creative turn when, not long after the Mishap, the Master had secured a corner on coffins and Haggerty had undertaken, with a little persuasion, to refit the kitchen. The pine was indeed handsome, and Haggerty rose to the challenge of conversion. At first he stacked the coffins on their sides and hinged the lids; but these lids, or doors as they had become, had a tendency either to flop open unexpectedly or to slam down on fingers. Haggerty ranged them vertically instead and fitted them with shelves. His system worked.

Greatly encouraged, he had gone on to make a bed of sorts from one of them that came up a little short. It did nicely for what later became Tots's sleeping quarters. With a little modification to suit the narrow angle of the wall, it fitted to perfection.

Scoria called him a weirdo.

"We never asked Haggerty," said Sherilee.

"He's too busy to sit here rabbitting on about birthdays." Mrs. Phelum could not do without Haggerty, not with the electricity rationed the way it was. "When's yours anyway?" She was looking at Scoria.

Tots, dejected, pushed her plate away. The conversation had spoiled her pie. She was not so much neglected as conscientiously ignored.

"The fifteenth of March."

"Beware the eyes," muttered Mildred into her cup.

Morgan scrunched out her cigarette. Fools. Coffee break was always exasperating. She began to gather the plates.

"Here, I'll do it," said Tots. Of whose birthday no one had enquired. She was used to being ignored but this was not the same. It was a flat-footed kindness, perversely cruel. For—as everyone knew—no one knew, exactly, when she was born. No one in fact knew very much about Tots at all. Including Tots.

She waited for the others to get back to work before she spoke. "Mrs. Phelum?"

"What?"

"Don't no one know when me birthday is?"

Mrs. Phelum frowned.

"No, ducks. Not exactly."

"But it's December, innit?"

"You've asked that before."

"Well, innit?"

"Yes. I suppose."

"An I'm thirteen?"

"Maybe."

"Don't you know?"

"Thirteen years is a long time. It might just as well be twelve, or eleven—or fourteen. I can't remember."

"Didn't no one write it down?"

"No. Why should they?"

Yes, thought Tots. *Why should they?*

"I ain't nothin' to no one, am I?"

Mrs. Phelum turned round.

"I like you, ducks. Well enough."

"But you never writ it down."

"No. I never." Guilt, reflected Mrs. Phelum, was not dissimilar to a half-digested lump of bread lodged somewhere high behind the breast-bone. "Haven't you got your indentures?" she said. "They'll tell you."

"Me what?"

"Your indentures."

Tots, suspicious, cast her eyes down and felt around her teeth with her tongue, confirming that they were indeed her own.

"Your indentures. What they gave you when they took you on— like when you was a baby. A contract. Like. A certificate."

"A piece of paper?"

"Ah, the light come one."

"All tore down one side?"

"Sort of. They torn it down the middle. You got one bit an' *he* got the other." She aspirated heavily, perhaps out of respect.

"Oh, yeah. I got that under me mattress."

In the scullery Scoria pricked up her ears. She had not known that Tots possessed anything other than her one or two clothes.

"There you are then," said Mrs. Phelum. "Seek an' ye shall find. Ask an' ye shall receive."

"Look under your mattress," called Scoria, "an' watch out for the fleas." She screeched with delight at her own wit. The sound, as if she had caught her finger in the mincer, reminded Tots to get out of range.

"But you're not goin' anywhere, sunshine. Not 'til you've swept up. You can start here," said Mrs. Phelum. "An' don't hang about."

The Pantry

S coria saw the snails and knocked them from the pantry shelf. They clattered lightly on the cracked tiles. "Tough titty, Tots," she said. For Tots would have to sweep them up. It was her job to sweep the House from the dry webby attic to the mouldering cellar. Tots swept not to keep the House clean (it was not, never had been and never would be), but because it was her place in life, a place she was happy to occupy; outside the House, unfortunates without a place were removed, cleared, at regular intervals. It was as well to know one's place and hang on to it. Jobs were no longer a consideration. There was only service. Finding and keeping a place was a national, an international, preoccupation, a place, that is, in the service of those who had never had the need to labour for their bread.

It was the very question of place that so rankled Scoria, not for its life and death significance but because, ever since she had been promoted, she had resented hers. Since the Mishap that had all but wiped North America from the face of the earth, dust had become a permanent feature of the world's weather. It was America's only export, arriving in Europe in intermittent storms to settle softly on the decaying cities. That did indeed beg to be interred. Its level of accumulation on the dome of the Greenwich Observatory was daily recorded. It gave the people something to do. Moving it here and there had been Scoria's job. And then Tots had taken it and she, Scoria, had been promoted; now a Class Five Domestic, she scrubbed. Government, reliably inept, had placed scrubbing above sweeping in the Job Descriptions scale, placed the pain of reddened knuckles scraping the bottom of charred pans above the airy delights of miniature clouds wafting about the ankles. Promotion had not made Scoria gracious. The look in her eyes suggested that while her hands scoured the pans her mind was rubbing out fellow humans. The pans were the only items in the house that gleamed.

Scoria herself had slip-slopped her way beyond description. Words unravelled from her when she walked, trailed after her in long untidy strings of morose slovenliness, their frayed ends tangling in knots of unheard-of nastiness. No neat labels for Scoria. Descriptions fell apart on her jagged edges. Nor would she be salvaged.

Everything irritated Scoria and today nothing more so than the dead and dying snails. *In extremis* they had oozed a slightly iridescent blue-black gum over the cracked marble of the shelf. Scoria dragged her rag across it, leaving most of it behind but picking up enough of the bad smell to carry with her like an evil aura for the rest of the day. She stamped hard on a snail just for the scrunch of it and went back to what, in more comfortable times, would have been a utility room; in the absence of utilities it had undergone something of a regression to scullery. Scoria dumped one of the empty milk cans into the sink.

"I want them cans good as new," called Mrs. Phelum from the kitchen. "I shall want to see my face in them."

"Your face, my arse."

Milk cans. In the twenty-first century. She must be the only Class Five in London since the Mishap—or even since ninety years before the Mishap—who had ever had to clean milk cans. Oh there was still milk all right. The cows that were left were kept in maximum security the way racehorses used to be, but you could still get the stuff delivered—if you had the ready, and the Master was never short of that. Mrs. Phelum, though, she had to have her own four-legged dairy out the back: Lilly. The last Jersey cow in England, she called it. And who knew wherever else. Fed it on sacks of dog food, she did. Silly cow.

"Manners maketh the man," called back Mrs. Phelum, whom it was hard indeed to rile.

"Woman, if you're talking to me."

"Suit yourself." Easy Mrs. Phelum. No one rocked her boat, with its ballast of contentment. Takes all sorts, she would say, amiability rising, enveloping, like warm dough. She made Scoria boil.

Who now disgruntled started on the cans. Oh, to have her old job back again. Or better, to be doing Mildred's job. For she could hear the weedy Mildred, Kitchen Aid, in the kitchen now, lending her inept assistance with the plums, sending the pits skittering across the table and onto the floor. For Tots to sweep. It was a consolation.

"Cans!" Scoria said, and would have spat only that there were footsteps approaching from the garden; but it was Ben, she could tell, and since Ben was only nine she spat anyway.

"Excuse me," said Ben. (And had manners. It made her want to do it again.) "Do you know where Gordon's snails are?" Gordon was Ben's twin and quite unlike him. Gordon had a penchant for experimenting with life forms inferior—though perhaps only in size—to himself.

"On the floor."

"On the floor?" This was not altogether disheartening. The snails, Ben thought, might be in with a chance. "They'll get away."

"Wanna bet?" Scoria scoured harder, increasing the clanking in the sink, drowning little, inquisitive boys.

Of course not. Watching her, Ben realized they had never had a chance. Not that he had ever imagined he might save them. No, if his brother Gordon wanted something he usually got it, and Gordon wanted snails for the Day Out. He had planned to fatten them for the occasion; Ben had hoped only to supervise their demise, see to it that their ending was humane.

"Where are they?"

Scoria jerked her chin in the direction of the pantry.

"An' don't lay it on me," she called after him. Upsets with the sons—especially when Gordon was involved—had a habit of percolating to the father. "He forgot. That's all. They been dead for two days."

Ben stood at the pantry door and stared hopelessly at the remains of the snails. Lugging themselves around all their lives over rocks and sharp gravel and prickly grass, sheltering from acid rain, minding broken glass and looking out for the cat—who by rights should have been snatched for a quick meal long ago—all for this. To finish up as one of Gordon's failed experiments, to prove to anyone who wished to know (but nobody did, not even Gordon, who had lost interest) that snails fed on a diet of twenty-year-old raspberry jelly for a week will not metamorphose into pink delicacies in time to be served as a surprise at a birthday picnic.

"You squashed them," he said coming back. Which was a mistake.

Scoria whipped round and grabbed his shirtfront with red soapy hands.

"They smashed." Scoria had an old video of *The Untouchables* and modelled her behaviour accordingly. "They smashed, O.K.?"

"O.K.," said Ben, contracting his chest and wriggling free. He brushed the suds from his crumpled shirt and went on through to the kitchen.

Mrs. Phelum was pulling things out of a chicken.

"The snails are dead. We can't have snails," he announced.

"That's a relief, ducks."

"Gordon will be mad."

"Never mind Gordon. He'll be too busy feedin' his face with all this other stuff when we get there."

"What are we having?"

"Chicken."

"Is that all?" There was always chicken. Chicken and seagull. Perhaps because both were scavengers of a kind, one digging in the dirt, the other snatching at whatever came its way. Not unlike the Master, either of them.

The seagulls, that were all strangely mute and had come from no one knew where, had taken over from the pigeons that had once been so numerous; but seagulls were hard to catch and so more often than not it was chicken. Other meat was out of the question.

There was of course the odd occasion when something new turned up and if you were in the right place, behind the old bus station say, at the right time with something worth trading, you just might come home with a nice piece of brisket or some kidneys.

"An' patty," she encouraged (she was above French accents) "an' pork pies, an' scotch eggs," (never mind that they were chicken) "an' some cold tongue," (best not to ask) "headcheese and sausage rolls —" Mrs. Phelum's fingers found what they were looking for inside the chicken, "oh, and a pressed duck. Jacky caught it up the river. There's one or two come back, he says. Up by the old sewage plant."

Ben's stomach began to feel like a hot-air balloon rising, slowly.

"Anything else?" he asked.

"Anything else? Only enough to feed a navy. I been bakin' all week for this do and Jacky's been to the Outlet twice."

This was what Ben wanted to hear, for although the food industry had shut down along with all the rest, the Outlets were still crammed with old stocks of processed foods, the special preserve, now that they were finite, of the very rich, who plundered them avidly, regardless of the age or condition of the contents. Sell-by dates, stamped as they were on what had proved to be the last of such items, had acquired a new and ominous meaning, an eschatology all their own. 'The End' they might have read. Though it made no difference. In the way of all apocalyptic messages they were assiduously ignored, accorded the kind of fleeting attention formerly granted to news of dental check-ups or nuclear meltdowns. They were the new writing on the wall, obscene graffiti no one wanted to read.

"We got Pizza Pops, Weenios, instant pudding, an' Dreem Creem, some of them machos—"

"Nachos."

"That's them, Craquerettes, Cheezee Puffs, Frooty Loops, Chunkie Chooz and some chocolate marshmallows. An' we're gettin' some whatsits." She paused for approval.

Ben's colour had improved but he was not happy. Food was Mrs. Phelum's natural element and, the packages aside, she liked to be in it—grease on her fingers, peel on her toes, the smell of it, the feel of it, the flour of it in her hair. But it made Ben uncomfortable.

It was not that he was unused to such quantities. His father, an investment dealer, had access. His father had always had access. Ben was destined to inherit it. The Mishap—it was never referred to in any other way—changed nothing. When Ben's father witnessed the economic foundation of his world swept away, when he saw that all his electronic assets were as chaff in the wind, it had taken him less than an hour to turn things around; it was simply a matter, he realized, of moving real stocks, cereal boxes and light bulbs, where before he had moved numbers on a screen. It was a new and exhilarating kind of stock market and he was not the only one to play it. Foresight and speed of reaction still cost nothing. Voracity was still the prime mover. In a matter of days most of the available resources were once again in the hands of the few and Ben's father had sharpened the edge he already enjoyed. Within the House, a state of plenty continued to prevail. What disturbed Ben was his recent and unpleasant realization that access was limited, an elite prerogative, though he did not put it in those terms. Outside the House, life was not a bowl of cherry pudding. He could not understand how Mrs. Phelum could smack her lips in the face of such knowledge.

Mrs. Phelum on the other hand found such satisfaction in the stockpiling itself, in the preservation and the preparation of food, that its consumption was almost an afterthought and her enjoyment was without guilt. It did not do at all to cry over spilt milk or empty vessels, she said, just because your cup was brimming over. Permutations on proverbs were her forte. Moreover, while she would have given any amount of food to any honest face at the door and no questions asked, it simply was not her style to let the rumour of shortages and hardships outside the House detract from the fact of a nice dish of chicken à la King with Chinese noodles.

But Ben's protective coat of innocence was wearing thin. He could not bear the bold-faced groaning of the board. *Embarras de richesse* indeed. It was the reason Jacky the Lackey was compelled to run through the streets as he tore back from the Outlet with a loaded cart. It was the reason some of the lackeys were armed.

"That's a lot, isn't it?" Ben asked, tentative.

"It'll tide us over till supper."

Ben still was not sure. He wished adults would signal their jokes more clearly. If they were jokes.

"Is everyone going?"

"Everyone."

"Even Tots?"

"Even Tots."

Tots's Room

W hile Tots swept up the snails, Mrs. Phelum read out the rest of the work orders to her. Tots itched. She could not wait until midday to get to her room and out of Scoria's way.

Work orders for the domestics came down, or out, each day on a dotty printout from the still-room at 5:58 am. After reading the orders and snuffing with superiority once or twice, Mrs. Phelum would copy them in smudgy pencil and with her own modifications onto the back of an envelope and pin them to the cork apron of her black mammy on the wall. She was very fond of this plastic icon—it had a red and yellow spotted kerchief—and she did not know at all why Jacky, who after all had an aunty in Trinidad, should call her a fascist, whatever that was. Jacky often bewildered her, but then he wrote poems so that probably explained it.

"Side steps, back steps," she read.

"Right," said Tots, disgruntled but managing not to show it. She was always sweeping steps or stairs.

Besides the usual deposit of grey dust, officially termed 'weatherdust' as if it were a gift of nature, the side steps leading up from the scullery were covered with a thick sanding of brick dust as a result of recent attempts to pin the wall.

Tots tied a grubby handkerchief over her mouth and set about moving medium-sized clouds of it down consecutive steps. At the bottom she rested. Her arms and legs prickled with the dust. But even as she stood looking at her work, she felt a sudden movement on the face of the wall above her and looking up saw that every join between every brick had begun to leak. A thousand tiny waterfalls of dust. She ducked, just as the Government jet mounted the roof, or seemed to, before it disappeared, an avenging pterodactyl out for a quick lunch. She shut her eyes and put her hands over her ears while the air cracked.

The wall, when she looked up again, was still there and so were the waterfalls, trickling to a standstill to the crackle of the fading roar. Tots hurried round to the back before anyone could suggest the steps had not been swept.

The steps at the back of the house led up to what used to be a back door but had long ago been bricked over. Tots liked to sit on the steps there when she could. It was flanked on one side by a high wall, behind which were the Mistress's ivy-hung apartments and her private courtyard, surrounded by a brick wall and covered with a pergola that, winter and summer, supported a dense canopy of foliage.

Tots enjoyed sweeping these steps in summer, with the bubble and squeaking of the babies on the other side, or the voice of the Mistress, sounding quite unlike herself, fruity and happy. Tots liked to sit and listen. But not today. She finished as fast as she could, shoved the dust into some nettles and made it back through the kitchen without further attention from Mrs. Phelum, who was fully occupied with the neckwear of a Seventh Day Adventist prostrated by the heat.

The door to Tots's room was in the passage outside the kitchen just at the point where the main staircase, ascending from the front entrance hall, reached the back wall and turned to continue its ascent. Here a door opened to reveal not only the usual brooms and dustpans but a second, narrow flight of stairs, an inner staircase, small and rickety, nested under the main staircase and leading up to an attic-like space beneath it.

In this space there was just room enough for Tots's customized bed. When she stretched out on the thin, crunchy mattress, she could touch any wall, not to mention the inverted stairs hanging above her. A hole for a priest, or a terrorist. It had been used before.

A window had been set in the apex of the triangular wall. Tots could see clouds when she lay in bed, sometimes the moon. If she stood on the edge of the cot she could just glimpse a rocking ocean of plum tree breaking over the wall next door. It hadn't bloomed for years after the Solid Winter and then one spring it was back, the blossom whipped to white foam. When Tots looked out of the window she might have been in a boat. She might even have been going somewhere. As soon as she reached her room, Tots closed the door and went straight to the bed.

The indentures were there under the pallet, one half of a piece of legal bond, the whole having been torn roughly down its length at approximately the centre. It was water-marked with tea-coloured stains and bore the inked print of a small foot. Tots liked the foot. Years ago it had been the foot that had induced her to preserve the document though she had no way of guessing at its meaning. *When you was a baby.* Tots supposed that it was her foot that had been pressed to the paper.

She could recognize her name. It was there at the top. TOTS. Two trees on either side of a pond and a snake removing itself from the scene. The rest was as unintelligible as Mildred's tea-leaves, for Tots could not read.

She removed the paper and sat down on the bed. Her forefinger travelled along the smooth edge and down the tear on the other side. Slowly she traced her name. Then she closed her eyes. It might not have been there at all. She put the paper on the floor, took off her battered running shoe and placed her bare foot over the tiny inked one with its five round peas. It fitted perfectly under the arch of her own, sheltered. A child, a cave. An obligation to build a fire. To light up the dark.

THIS INDENTURE made this
the year of our Master two tho

    BETWEEN:
               TOTS

hereinafter named "the said To
OF THE ONE PART
AND:
           THE RIGHT HONC

of the Borough of Pimlico
hereinafter named "the said Ma
OF THE OTHER PART

    WHEREAS the said Master
the Misplaced Persons Act has
exercise lawful guardianship
over the person rights and eft
    AND WHEREAS the said Tot
subject to the just stewardshi
effects right privileges and cl
the said Tots and does acknowl
willingly and without compunct
    AND WHEREAS the duties obl
upon the said Tots shall be deer
accordance with the exercise of
    THEREFORE the said Tots i
enfeo legally bound beholden ar
heirs and assigns for his sole
from this the seventy-seventh da
Master two thousand and twenty
    IN WITNESS WHEREOF this s
do hereunder set their hands

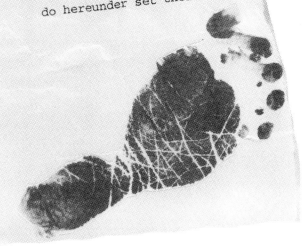

The Front Hall

V irginia Pinnacle clicked across the black and white tiles and stopped in front of the hallstand. Like the Master, her husband, Mrs. Pinnacle wore suits. Uncompromisingly tailored, their tubular sleeves in close formation, they were ranked hanger after hanger in her wardrobe, the vase-shaped bodices, the cylindrical skirts, like so much empty armature awaiting the challenge of her pear-shaped flesh. Perma-pressed into service, these were suits which, with some chunks of gilt at wrist or neck and a sturdy bra beneath, could be counted on to confront the world. There was a suit to seduce members of the Board and one to intimidate domestics, a suit to dazzle the archbishop twice a year at services in the new riot-proofed cathedral and (one's friends being not always as robust as oneself) several in black for the funerals that occurred considerably more frequently than twice a year, that were, in fact, predictably thick on the ground, thick as flies you might say, as each new virus mutated; there were two or three in slubbed silk for cocktails with diehards like oneself, two in wool that had been for travelling and which were allowed to remain as souvenirs of glittering foyers in Brussels or New York, and there was a dun-coloured one in polyester for visiting the sick and having one's hairpiece cleaned.

The suit selected for duty today was airforce-blue tweed and had shoulders like landing pads. The tweed, with occasional white hairs sticking out from it, gave the Mistress a whiskery look, as if, Tots always thought, she had inadvertently sat in the cat's basket. It was a prickly sort of thing, a suit to command prompt service, correct change, and an unfair advantage at the Fuel Ration Office, where Mrs. Pinnacle always entered the blue cord maze at 'Exit' and still emerged against all the odds unscathed.

Mrs. Pinnacle was already hot but did not let it show as she presented herself to the hallstand for inspection. The glass no longer hung vertically in its supports but leaned out from the top, curiously foreshortening its subject and endowing the skull with abnormally large frontal lobes, which Mrs. Pinnacle chose to ignore. She tugged smartly at the hem of her jacket. In view of the weather, she thought better of the banana-yellow gloves and decided instead to clutch them, like a spare pair of flippers, against her handbag. Or gauntlets.

She turned sideways to check her profile and caught sight of Tots standing in the shelter of the dusty elephant grass that leaned out brokenly from the umbrella stand. "You?" she said.

Tots could not think of a reply that did not sound impolite.

"Nothing to do?"

"Yes, Ma'am. I got lots—"

"Then?"

"I was wonderin' if I could see you a minute. Or two."

"Well hurry up." Mrs Pinnacle looked at her watch.

"Um, I was thinkin' maybe if I could talk to you private. Like."

Mrs. Pinnacle's lower jaw executed a little motion of its own, as if it had just been filled with lumpy potato. She sighed raspily.

"Come in here," she said and led the way into the library. Every room in the House had its smell. You could walk through blindfold, stop at any point and name the exact location. The library's smell was a complex wet-dry combination. It competed with the alcoholic perfume the Mistress wore. She was already looking at her watch again.

"Mrs. Pinnacle, Ma'am. I've give good service now for—as long as I can remember," again that sigh, like a shovelful of frosty snow, "and I'm not askin' no favours but there's somethin' as I'd like to know."

"Well?"

"Me name, Ma'am."

Mrs. Pinnacle, her cheeks sucked in tight, shook out the spare pair of flippers and began to pull them on, finding as she did so the words for her exasperation, one short burst for each tug:

"Now—I have—as you know—a great deal of demands—made on my time—and if you—"

"I'm not havin' you on, Ma'am. I mean it. I'm fed up bein' just Tots. I have to have another name, everyone does, an' I was thinkin' as you might know what it is." She pushed her case a little further, "Perhaps."

"I screen the staff who work here, naturally. But you, I believe, were what is known as a foundling."

"So who found me?"

"I'm afraid I was busy at the time. I don't recall. I believe there was some mention of the milkman."

She returned her attention to the gloves, pressing, pressing between each finger as if she did indeed fear to grow webs between. She seemed particularly ill at ease. Tots was fascinated, never having seen her mistress so unmistressy.

"Weren't there anythin' with me? Didn't I have no papers? Nothing?"

"Young lady, I don't think you quite understand. A mother abandoning her child on a doorstep in London in the middle of winter would hardly be so foolish as to leave her name and telephone number."

"Well what about me indentures?"

The muscles of Mrs. Pinnacle's face drew towards the bridge of her nose, where they formed an indignant question mark.

Tots took advantage of the silence and ploughed on. "Someone's got to have the other half. An' if you don't mind, Ma'am, I'd like to have a look at it."

"The other half?"

"Yes, Ma'am."

"But if you already have your half I don't see how the rest of it can possibly be any concern of yours. I suggest you get back to your work."

"Now if you'll excuse me—I shall be late for my appointment." With which she opened her handbag, checked in it for nothing at all, snapped it shut and took her blue prickly self off and out of the front door.

Oh excuse you! thought Tots. Ain't no one to excuse you, Missus, no one. Call yourself a human being! You wouldn't have no trouble impersonatin' a tailor's dummy, you wouldn't. Perhaps you *are* a dummy, runnin' on microchips an' you walked right out the shop. Bit of a shock, real life, innit? Bet you can't wait for someone to switch you off so's you won't have to bother speakin' to us *people* no more.

It always cheered Tots to indulge in a spot of virulence. She heaved a great sigh; and there was nothing frosty or blasted about it. It was a summer's day, a cliff-top drop, free-as-the-wind, heart-like-a-bird, warm-sea-breeze sigh. She did it again. But the bird had flown.

The Library

T he library was oppressive. There was an electric chandelier but the bulbs had gone and no one had replaced them. Tots, when she went in to sweep, always wanted to pull open the velvet curtains which protected the books from the sun, but they were so frayed and rotted she knew they would come down. There was a large carved oak desk, with a wonky leg that stood on two volumes of *Cassel's History Of The Franco-Prussian War*. And there was a small computer. Tots had switched it on once but it had said, in an officious voice, "Please do not operate when the count exceeds the Safe Daily Average." So she had switched it off.

She listened to Mrs. Pinnacle's heels striking the tiles on the way to the front door. The library's double-decker smell reasserted itself. Uppermost in the air was an odour sharp and pungent. It was the smell of newspaper scorched in the sun, words so tinder-dry they might ignite at a glance. But underlying the scent of danger was the source of the oppression, the hopeless smell of wet carpet, thick like humus. And this heavier smell too must have originated with the books for it clearly did not belong to the threadbare remnants of Persian carpet that in places showed the floorboards through its pattern.

Alone now in the middle of this dingy, musty room, surrounded by row upon row of dusty books, Tots was cowed. The pressure of the enormous stockpiles of energy massed in the wads of paper was palpable. She was crumpling. Compressed between the dark covers were the endless permutations of the alphabet, the DNA of thought, the very stuff of it encoded and organized so that you could pick it up, put it down, slip it under your pillow, give it away to a friend.

And perhaps not only thought. But life itself. All the thrills, the spills, the ups and downs, the next episode, it was all there. So they said. It'll make you laugh, it'll make you cry. You'll never be the same once you LEARN TO READ.

You can do it! Step across the border to SUCCESS! Between these very covers countless successful men and women have charted the courses of their lives, signalled the turnings they took, not to mention the ones they didn't but could have. Share their secrets. It's up to you! Tired of the same old realm of possibility? Enter the delirious whirl of action penned by the nibs of the famous, the men and women who had Drive, Determination, Initiative. Men and women with Vision. They didn't ask Mrs. Pinnacle when they wanted something. They got up and took it, or did it. Or found it. Whoever they were.

Whatever it was.

Tots made up her mind there and then that she would learn to read. She would find the other half one way or another and then she would learn to read. Or perhaps she ought to learn to read first.

Or how would she know what she had found? The idea glowed from the shadows. She put down her broom and went over to the shelves.

She might have been Eve, reaching out. But the spine of the first book came away in her hand. At once there was a pattering and something scrambled behind the row of books, then silence.

Tots pulled at another, and another. The spines all came away, trailing strands of linen and flakes of glue and setting free an unmistakable, pungent odour. Heaps of milled paper fell back where once there had been pages.

She moved along the row. Again the pattering, this time panicked, and a blind scrabbling back and forth, a rodent alarm that set up wave after wave of movement behind the books at every level.

Tots, caught up in the excitement, ran after the sounds, pulling at the books randomly. Spines, covers, all came away loose in her hands, sometimes whole sections, their backs glued together by the pressure of years and a potent mix of mouse pee.

The shredded paper they left behind fell in mounds, the black letters of the print indistinguishable from the seeds of excrement scattered among them.

"What are you doing?"

Had she been about to connect with twenty thousand volts Tots could not have snatched her hand away from the books more quickly.

But it was Ben.

"Gawd, Ben! You scared the lights out of me."

"Sorry. What are you doing?" Ben was amiable.

"Shut that door will you. I'm goin' in for rodent control. Here, look at this." She hooked a book away. "Mice. See? They been through the whole lot."

Ben stirred the soft nest of the pages. "I wonder if they know what they've been eating."

"It's criminal."

"No. No one ever reads them. Not even Jacky."

"Well I was going to."

Ben looked at Tots. It wasn't like her to lie. "You can't read."

"I know that. I was going to ask you to teach me, wasn't I?"

"Me? I don't much like reading. Except poems. They're O.K. You can remember them. And I suppose it's useful sometimes, reading. You can learn the names of birds they used to have and stuff like that. It—"

But Tots was no longer by his side. He turned round. She was over at the shelves on the next wall pulling the remains of book after book, sniffing uncontrollably and gulping, her shoulders shaking. Ben minded her misery, incomprehensible as it was. He went to her.

"Don't cry."

"I'm tryin' not to, ain't I? I can't find one, not one. They're all ate to pieces."

"What do you want to learn to read for?"

"I just do, that's all."

Ben was not convinced. She relented.

"I want to know when I was born. That's why. An' who had me."

"Well, you're not going to find out from these. You need your birth certificate. What's your name?" Ben had never before thought to ask. Tots stared at him, her lips primped shut.

"Tots what?" he asked gently. "Don't you know?" But there was no coaxing the lips. It seemed suddenly unnecessary to persist. "Look, never mind. I'll teach you a poem."

As if it might be an answer.

"Now?"

As if it might be the answer.

"If you like."

Tots wiped the back of her forearm across her runny nose. For a moment Ben could not think of a single poem.

It was in the library before the mice had begun in earnest that Ben had taught himself to read. At the age of three, seeking refuge from his twin who hurled metal objects at his head and sometimes bit, he had discovered the library mouldering majestically in a room off the front hall. Hiding in there, he would open and close book after book, admiring the clever arced flight of the pages as they reassembled into a block. The sound of birds' wings. Little breezes blew on his chin. Pleasant as the experience was, it lacked profundity and Ben's eyes, seeking pattern in complexity, rested again and again on the minute black runes that covered the yellow paper. He was patient.

He sat for what may have amounted to days, staring at the letters that evinced a tolerance of their own, waiting, ranged, silent, for him to notice them—not jumping up and down for attention when his eyes rested on the preceding group, not clutching out to him as he moved on, but waiting—he had checked this—even inside the book in their appointed order, even when there was no one there to behold them. Ben so admired the letters that eventually they began to yield their secrets.

He perceived similarities and patterns, sometimes relationships, and when one day he found an illustrated encyclopaedia they finally spoke to him—not, to be sure, in any original fashion at first, they were nothing but his own words as he named the pictures for himself. But they spoke. And Ben marvelled at the voice which was not quite his but was no one else's either. Here was a voice that was liberated from all human chords, a written voice; it did not threaten or cajole, was never exasperated, or condescending, or touchy, or tricky, never dread as in Come here, or Goodnight. More marvellous still, in time and with practice the voice detached itself from his thought entirely and named him the names of things he had not known before. Unheard of names it spoke to him. It pronounced the foreign and articulated the wonderful. It told him secrets, made the unknown known. It was other.

Quickly he progressed from captions to text—and faltered, for although he had grasped all the concepts he needed to master single words, he had overlooked an elementary principle concerning the order of these single words, their proper progression from left to right when strung one behind the other along a line. He might indeed have foundered altogether had it not been for poetry:

fruitfulness mellow and mists of Season

Nothing was more beautiful. Ben saw no need for further reading. Here was all truth, all beauty. The rest of the library was hugely, ponderously superfluous.

And yet he came back. And back again. Seduced by the music, addicted to the mystery, he could not leave the poems alone. At last, remembering for Tots, he began:

"Night other the Eternity saw I
    light endless and pure of Ring great a Like
    bright was it as calm All
    years days hours in Time"

He stopped. "I can't remember any more."
"Well I got one an' it makes more sense than that.

"Solomon Grundy
Born on Monday

Christened on Tuesday
Married on Wednesday
Took ill Thursday
Worse on Friday
Died on Saturday
Buried on Sunday
This is the end of Solomon Grundy."

They looked at each other, dissatisfied.

"I'll teach you to read," said Ben. "I promise."

Tots rolled her lips tight against her teeth, trying not to loose control again. And then she was herself.

"Here," she said. "Help me put these rotten things back, will you?"

When the books were all ranged as neatly as their peeling spines would allow, Tots took her broom, swept the evidence from the shelves and glancing quickly round delivered it down the air vent with one expert flourish.

The Master Bedroom

W hen the door knob finally turned, when at last it clicked and released and the door actually moved to open, Tots thought she might be sick. But it would tone in. The Master's carpet, Tots remembered, was the clotted muddy colour of eel pie. They had taken it up once for a spring-cleaning and Tots had been called in to sweep up underneath. She had been busy brushing the grape pips and the toenail clippings into a tidy mound when the shiny black, squeakless shoes had appeared in the doorway. Powerless to speak or to look up, Tots had continued sweeping, her mind trapped under the shoes, her only thought that the socks inside housed the toes the clippings of whose nails she was then shepherding around the floor. She had felt sick then too.

With her hand still on the door knob for fear the spring would ping, she closed her eyes and made an act of will, addressed (unlike the Acts of Faith, Hope, Charity, and, most of all, Contrition she had learned from Father Terence) to herself. *O Tots, you can do it. You know you can. Go on, Tots. Go on, girl, do it. No lookin'. Just do it.* And she went in, closed the door behind her and opened her eyes.

Oh, the opulence. She resisted the urge to genuflect. The sheer mass and solidity of it was enough to make you toe the scratch, had you thought of doing otherwise. Here was nothing broken or makeshift, nothing out of kilter. This furniture was solid and grave, would never have the bad breeding to wobble, far less fall apart. No failures in here, oh no. The massive wardrobe, the dressing table and the tallboy stood transfixed by their own upright qualities. A troop of grunting moving men would never move these pieces. The bed itself, a four-poster, was the size of a small semi-detached and draped like a funeral parlour. Or a confessional.

Father Terence's had been a portable with curtains of the same purple brocade. He used to come round every Saturday (the Master had some other arrangement now, something like a season ticket as far as Tots could make out—she was not eligible) and set up his fold-out box, like a puppet theatre, on the dining room table, which would be covered for the occasion with a floor length cloth of black-out material from an old war. Spared in this way the unpleasantness of the church, which was usually full of addicts, the members of the Household could file comfortably in and out of the dining room, posting their sins in his ecclesiastical mail box, relieving themselves.

Tots, who had been given a rudimentary Catholicism for no reason she could ever determine, took part in the Saturday ritual. The memory of it was laced with adrenalin; there was no forgetting the blind curtain, how she watched it, waiting, wondering whether he was really there on the other side, hoping it might be her lucky day and he had gone for a cigarette. But he never had. It was the same every Saturday. Only worse. In the act of confessing she found it hard not to begin accusing the prosecution and defending herself. "I said I already swept out the coal shed but I never. I mean I was goin' to do it the day after anyways. Sort of. How could I do it with Lilly in there? Some of them work orders don't make no sense. An' you can't blame Mrs. Phelum. She just reads them out. It's *him*. He makes them up and he don't know what he's talkin' about. Oh an' I called him a silly prick again. Not to his face of course. An' nobody heard ...." The urge to justify was pathological. It was painful to suppress it. Soon she found it more efficient to begin the process of vindication before the act of confession. Her list of sins grew considerably shorter each week. Until at last there was nothing to confess and Tots was left with a free half hour on a Saturday morning and a lasting fear of any unseen presence.

The curtains of the bed, Tots noticed now, were closed. The hair at the nape of her neck began to tickle. Was he ....? He couldn't be. The thought appalled, enthralled. She had to know. In awful fascination she dropped to her hands and knees and began slowly to creep across the carpet. Once she thought she heard breathing, but it was only the soft scuffing of her knees. She stopped at the side of the bed and listened. *Bless me Father for I am about to sin.* It is about two seconds before I open the curtains, lift the lid, drop the clanger .... Holding one of the purple tassels (it might have been the fuse on a barrel of gunpowder) between her finger and thumb, she carefully lifted it (oh, don't go off) and peered underneath.

But the great bed was not occupied. Which was not to say that it was empty. In fact it was quite full. Try as she might Tots could not impose any order or meaning on the jumble of assorted rubber and leather items that were heaped upon the bed. "No wonder his room's so tidy," she thought. "He stuffs it all in here." Though where he would otherwise have stored this strange assortment she could not imagine. Some of it clearly belonged in the Mistress's room. And there was something that looked as if it ought to be kept downstairs and used at milking time. There was even a goat's head—which gave her a nasty turn—with an open mouth and a long ropey beard. But she did not have time to waste on any of this. She withdrew from beneath the purple fringe and stood up. There was nothing for her in the wardrobe or the tallboy—she looked. The clothes were all properly stacked, hung, layered, ranged, folded and piled: two dozen suits ploughing the colour spectrum all the way from not-quite-black to black; a dark harvest of socks at rest in a drawer all to themselves; everything in order and no loose ends anywhere.

It was when she opened the smaller drawers where most of the items were 44-carat that Tots began to realize the full implications of being the only appurtenance in the room that was not in its proper place. All this gentleman's hardware. She felt as if she'd been caught with half of it up her sleeve.

But there were no papers or documents of any kind.

Unless he kept them under his mattress.

Tots, in a hurry now, went back to the bed and got hold of a corner of the mattress.

"Well, well, well. Caught in the act. Red-handed."

Tots closed her eyes, wished she could close her ears, but this was Scoria's big moment and Scoria was not going to let it go.

"So. Little Hotsy-Totsy's got egg all over her face. Whaddya know? She'll have to do some pretty fast talkin' to get outta this one." She tilted her head. All the best cops were sardonic.

"Some pretty darn fast talkin'. Got a bedtime story ready for Big Daddy, have you? Got something in mind? You better, cause you're dead meat baby. Dead meat, less you can think one up pretty fuckin' quick."

"Oh shut-up," said Tots, who would not sink to fathom these implications. "I was lookin' for somethin'."

"Sure, baby. Tell that to the D.A."

"Who?"

"Never mind." Scoria sauntered over to the bed and drew back the curtain. She took a quick look, her eyes rollicking over the paraphernalia. A few things looked familiar. "My, my," she said. "You certainly found something didn't you. Oh, wouldn't he be pleased to know you've had an eyeful of this lot. Well, honey-bunch, whadd'll it be? You just dropped in to see what you could pick up in the way of the odd watch or the old cigarette case what nobody wants. Or you just come up to play with his toys?" She poked a rubbery-looking, globular item with her foot.

"Leave off," said Tots. "I told you I was lookin' for somefin'." She made to step past but found her way blocked.

Scoria, who would have preferred a wide-shouldered suit with big lapels, flexed the shoulders of her turquoise nylon work dress.

"I believe you," she said, "but *he's* not going to." A vile smile slid from one ear to the other and retreated. "Not if he ever finds out. What you was doin' with his toys."

She picked up the goat's head and pushed the staring face suddenly at Tots, who recoiled and sat down abruptly on the edge of the bed. Grinning, Scoria drew back, hoisted her skirt, and stuck the goat's head between her legs, its face staring stupidly at Tots, its gummy tongue lolling, and Tots in horrible fascination staring back.

Tots had only one thought. She's barmy, off her rocker, she said to herself, and hoped this moment like all others would pass. But Scoria was not quite finished.

"Get the picture?" she said and, just to make sure, she stuck out her pelvis and jerked the head rapidly up and down liked a crazed BMX rider, which served to confirm Tots's suspicions but did little to clarify.

"He won't like it one bit. Not one bit. But then he won't have to know, will he? Not unless I tell him. An' I won't do that, will I? Not if you're a good girl. You could manage to wash a few old pots couldn't you? Just to help out a friend. An' if I was to say I was a bit strapped one week, you could find a quid or two, no trouble, couldn't you? To help me out, I mean."

Not on your nelly, thought Tots. "Anythin' you say," she said fervently. "I will. I promise."

"I knew you'd see sense," said Scoria, dropping the goat's head and kicking it aside. If she'd had a fedora she would have dusted it off and put it on with a single sharp twist as she walked to the door. But she didn't.

The Scullery

It was late when Ben, unable to sleep, came creeping down to the kitchen to find something to eat. When Ben wanted to tiptoe only one leg co-operated; the other, injured at birth, lagged, so that the sound of Ben's attempt at silence was a loud *Ssh—ssh—ssh*.

But there was no one to notice. Mildred had gone off to bed with a hot water bottle and something coming on. She did not know what but her glands were up. Mrs. Phelum was asleep in front of the muttering range, her tea suspended in her tilted cup. Electricity had long been misered up and grudgingly metered out and so Mrs. Phelum, bereft of appliances, would at last tire. Not that she minded a more direct approach to her food. It was all her pleasure to cudgel and bludgeon it into submission with heavy wooden implements, to quarter, hack, slice and dice it with an assortment of surgical-looking knives before she fed it to the coal-black range, her big, tame, sexy pet of sultry liver and smoking lights.

This range, splendidly embellished beneath the grime with bunches of grapes and sheaves of corn, extended almost halfway along one wall and was equipped with an impressive array of doors and drawers. It was here, when she had baked or boiled the daily cartload of provisions, that Mrs. Phelum chose to sit at the end of the day, her fat thighs apart, the heat of the fire penetrating between, and she gazing through the open doors to the smouldering embers within. No one, least of all Mrs. Phelum, paused to think what would happen when, the last mince pie baked, the last stick of wood should be consumed. Summer and winter the beast was fed so that it roared steadily all of the day and part of the night, during the rest of which it purred sootily—while Mrs. Phelum dreamed of butter mountains and grainstorms and how to render them in sixteen individual portions.

It was only when Ben was cutting a second doorstep from the loaf (made from the musty, moth-infested flour that Mrs. Phelum said cost a bomb so you should think yourself lucky and don't complain) that he recognized the sniffs coming from the scullery. Tots, caught now in the grip of injustice with her hands in the washing-up, could do nothing but sniff.

"Is that you, Tots?"

"Who else do you think it is?"

"But what are you doing? Where's Scoria?"

"She fell under a bus."

"Really?"

Tots was at once refreshed to hear such honest pleasure. "No, not really. She won't ever come to no harm. Not Scoria. Here, dry up."

She handed Ben a sour grey tea-towel and he joined her at the sink, which was magnificent in greasy granite, wide and deep and sometimes used for bathing babies or strays. Tots herself had wiggled her toes in its ample trough when she was just a mewling mite, had sat in it and bumped her head on the tap, had even encountered her first and last Christmas turkey there, shared her bath with it, large, mute lump that it was, its chilly flesh surprising her into silence, puzzling her with its whiteness, which reflected her own but was a good deal more pimply. Or had she been waiting for the inevitable head (for didn't all creatures have one?) to eject perhaps and address her, to prophesy perhaps the Mishap that was about to happen, that was only round the corner, like a box of starred and striped fireworks waiting to go off.

"She's off gallivantin'," she said. "Havin' fun. But I tell you one thing. She better make the most of it, 'coz I'm not stickin' around here much longer. I've had it. I'm off."

"You're running away?"

Again that note of undisguised pleasure, this time charged with excitement. A happening. Action, lights, camera, obscura, secrets, intrigue. Until he realized.

"But I was going to teach you to read."

For Tots the notion of regret was novel. It would have to be considered. But not now. "Won't be time. It was bad enough before but now it's terrible. I'm in big trouble, Ben. Listen, don't tell no one?"

Right then Ben would have promised a limb, his lame one anyway, for a taste of this adventure. "Of course not."

"Well, she caught me in you dad's bedroom. Without me broom."

Ben was immobilized. Tots took a saucepan lid from his hand and replaced it on the pile.

"I told you it was bad."

"What was she doing there?"

Tots, who had been prepared to explain her own presence, had to think. It was not a question she had asked herself. She loved Ben all the more for asking it. And the shadow of regret began to assume a more definite shape.

"*I* dunno," she said. "I think it's more like what was *I* doing there."

"What were you doing?" Even Ben would have to ask in the end.

"Looking for something important. A piece of paper."

"Of my father's?"

"Not exactly. I mean it kind of belongs to me, an' all. I've already got one bit. It's got me name on it. I was going to get you to read it to me when I got the rest of it. From him I mean. They fit together, see. But I never found it."

"Where's your piece?"

"Here."

She pulled out the plug and dried her hands on her skirt. "It's a bit damp," she said, drawing the crumpled paper from her pocket.

Ben smoothed it out and they went outside on the steps where it was cooler.

They sat down in the light of the scullery window with the scent of nettles and night and the cabbage stench of the drain and Ben laid the paper on his knees and began to read.

"*this made indenture This—thou two Master our of year the—between—Tots—*' wait a minute, '*said the named herinafter—*' It looks as if it might be written backwards. They're always doing that." Ben the worldly, Ben the shrewd. He took it up again, this time from left to right, "*Of the one part and the Right Hono—of the Borough of Pimlico in the—hereinafter named the said—*' It still doesn't make any sense. And it doesn't have the rest of your name." He sighed. "You need the other half."

"Brilliant, Ben. That's brilliant."

He smiled. Sarcasm always glanced from Ben's helmet of innocence. She would not otherwise have used it.

"Thank you," he said. "What's it for, anyway?"

"Mrs. Phelum says it's a contract, like. For service."

"Well, you better not run away if my father has the other half."

Tots felt she had known this all along. She had only needed someone to say it. The paper had to do with more than meaning. It had to do with power.

She was out of her depth, but Ben waded in deeper, spearing a meaning here, a significance there:

"*—lawful guardianship—person rights and—just stewards—effects rights privileges—.*'" He paused. "*legally bound beholden and enfeo—.*'"

A siren sounded somewhere and Roger the cat yowled an unholy greeting to one of his boyfriends, but Ben did not look up.

"*enfeo?*" He was stumped.

The boyfriend yowled back.

"Oh, I get it." As if it were a clever joke. "You can't run away and leave him while he still has the other half. *That's* why you were looking for it."

The two cats tore through the rubbish at the bottom of the garden and came out half way up. In the darkness they were a whiplash, nothing more. Up the wall and over. Gone.

"It is now," said Tots.

Scoria's Room

U p in her room, Scoria was getting dressed to go out. So was
Eliott Ness. She had a video tape of a single episode of *The
Untouchables,* a recording of a rerun of the original and she
watched it on an ancient black and white portable. It gave the ac-
tors a murky look entirely appropriate to the underworld. How
Scoria had acquired the video or the machine or had been allowed
to pirate the electricity to run it was a mystery to the other members of the House, though Mrs. Phelum said that nothing would
surprise her. Nothing. Scoria herself would never tell. The Master
had given it to her not so much in payment for services rendered
as in plight for silence. Had Scoria been as sharp as she appeared,

she might have acquired substantially more than a video machine, for the Master's misconduct down among the dishrags had been considerable. But, dishonest as she was in almost every other respect, she had, when asked what it was she most wanted, succumbed to an unprecedented attack of candour and replied promptly, "I wanna watch telly again and see *The Untouchables*."

The palms of the Master's hand then had stopped sweating. He was torn only between making it seem more attractive to her, so as to cement the idea, and getting it done straight away before she changed her mind.

"A telly of your very own?" he murmured, tucking in his shirt.

"Right."

"I'll see what I can do. Meanwhile, we wouldn't want—"

"'Anyfin' to get around, now would we?' No, we wouldn't. It'd ruin me reputation."

The Master saved his anger until next time and Scoria got her video.

She kept one eye on it now as she dressed. She liked denim and zips. Her underwear was best kept out of sight, being a palish grey and sprouting little worm ends from the wavy elastic. Her green sleeveless sweater and denim skirt, all slits and holes, some intentional, some not, did their best to reveal it, but she had a black vinyl jacket, with zips, and though it was still warm out she put it on. It was her friend; she felt vulnerable without it.

Eliott Ness shrugged his jacket on over his shoulder holster. Off for another night of larks on the mean streets, where she wouldn't mind blowing away a few people herself. Even a spiked verbal exchange would be something, should she be so lucky. She wondered sometimes what she did wrong. She had all the right answers: 'Who d'you think you're talkin' to?' and 'What's it to you?' She even had some of the openers: 'Oi you, dickhead!' and 'Got your eyeful?' but they never had the effect she hoped for, which was something along the lines of mortal combat. Instead the recipient would simply shrug, or worse, might turn away and talk to someone else as if she had said nothing at all. It made Scoria wonder why she bothered; sometimes she kept to her room for months. Her room was painted black. It helped. She could savour her choleric existence, could taste the rancour and the gall. Could watch telly, too. There on the murky box humans bumped up against each other and away on the easy castors of dialogue, rolled smoothly from set to set through the plot until they reached the theme music, which signified the eternity of rewind. It was better than the tapes that ran in her head, whether or not she wanted them to. Better than watching over and over the sneer on the Master's face as he waited for her to undress, or seeing again and again the ill-concealed displeasure that passed like a shadow behind people's eyes when she came into a room. Not that she was likely to let these things get on top of her. Years ago, escaping from the wreck of her mother's arms, watching from behind the broken furniture her mother being salvaged by a succession of divers who took the parts they wanted, came up for air, threw back the rest, she had concluded that spines were not a bad thing. Or claws.

Eliott was picking up his hat. He had a certain way of smiling (and who wouldn't, always on the winning team): nothing changed on his face but you knew what was happening inside. If Scoria tried it she looked as if she had a piece of silver paper stuck in a cavity.

She switched off the machine and decided she would walk through box town. She was a winner there.

The Terminal

L
ate as it was, Tots did not sleep when she went to bed. Instead she waited until she was reasonably sure that everyone else was asleep.

The door to the library stood open. She crossed the hall and went in, closing the door quietly behind her in the dark With her hands stretched out in front of her she sleepwalked herself to the library table and groped across it to the computer. The screen lit up at her touch casting a thin light into the room. The electronic voice emitted an imperious 'Bing,' simulating earlier models which had not had the power of speech.

An abstract pattern appeared on the screen and formed itself into the semblance of a man's face.

"*Yes?*"

Tots coughed. "Um. I'd like to learn to read—um, please—if it's O.K.?"

"*Certainly. Shall we begin?*" The smile on the man's face curled itself into a question.

"Uh—yes. Please."

Instantly the face disappeared and a short sequence of letters appeared on the screen.

"*What does this say?*" said the voice.

"Dunno."

"*Very good.*" The screen flashed and the word appeared again. "And this?"

"Dunno."

"*Very good. Now this.*" Two words appeared on the screen, the first and beside it, on the left, a new one.

"I dunno."

"*Very good. We shall pause for evaluation.*" A single word flashed onto the screen. "*Can you read this?*"

"No."

"*Very good.*" The word flashed and reappeared. "*Careful now. You must answer the next two questions correctly. Is this the same word?*"

"Looks like it."

"*Can you read it?*"

"No."

"*Excellent. We shall proceed to the next module.*"

"Eh?" said Tots.

"*Shall we proceed?*"

"If you want."

The screen changed again.

"*Here are two more words. Read them.*"

"I can't."

"*Very good. You are now ready for five words. Read them please.*"

"I told you I can't." Tots was sounding exasperated but the computer continued.

"*Very good. Now these.*"

"I told you I can't read nothin'," Tots continued, her words synchronising to the last syllable.

"Excellent. Your speed is improving. It is time for a mid-programme assessment." And before Tots could ask what that meant a new voice purled:

"The candidate's score is 100%. We wish the candidate every success in the completion of the programme." A string of five words appeared on the screen in a wreath of lilies and violets.

Tots was about to speak when she stopped and tallied the words she was about to say. And then she tested her thesis.

"You mean I can read?"

"Congratulations," said the first voice. *"You have just graduated. Here is your long text."* An entire passage came up on the screen:

> Don't gimme that. Think I'm stupid or
> somefin'? I come in here to learn to read, not
> to play silly buggers with a machine. You
> don't fool me that easy. You ain't taught me
> nothin'. Not sweet Fanny Adams. You're a
> disgrace you are, a disgrace to science and
> learnin'. You ought to be ashamed. Switch
> yerself off before I kick you in the works.

Tots didn't say a word. She looked ruefully at the jiggle of letters. It could have been the recipe for a Christmas pudding for all she knew. Eventually the words disappeared and were replaced by just two. "Clever Dick," Tots was about to say. And changed her mind.

"I'm going to bed," she said. And the light on the screen went out.

Top Storey

T ots rummaged in her box to find her sweater. Even in high
summer it was always cold at the top of the house. She
pulled it out and stuck her arms into it. It was pale blue and it had
so matted and thickened with washing that it resembled a small
blanket cut to her size and shape, its buttons aged to the colour of
unbrushed teeth. She kicked the box back under the bed, picked up
her broom at the bottom of the stairs and set off.

The quantities of dust which sometimes still fell in intermittent
showers were enough to keep Tots fully occupied in the rest of the
house and she had not been up to the top for years, which was just
fine by her, thank you very much. It freaked her out, gave her the

willies. But here was an opportunity. What only knocks once, Mrs. Phelum would say. Make hay, never look a gift horse. Tots had promised herself that she would search the House from top to bottom and here was her chance.

Top floor, the work order had said, and Mr. Hawkin's room. *Mr. Hawkin out,* Mrs. Phelum had pencilled in by way of encouragement, for Mr. Hawkin was commonly regarded as simple-minded and carried all unwitting about his smiling face the fears of others in a confused aura of danger. But Tots was not bothered one way or the other. She was interested in the unused rooms. She tried to think what was up there: old filing cabinets, a desk? She could not remember. Every time she went up there she came to some kind of grief and when she came down again her memory considerately erased the experience. She had for instance no recollection at all of her first visit except for the terrible, numbing cold. She did not like thinking about it.

There were seven rooms at the top of the House. They were reached by a flight of brown-carpeted stairs which joined a long narrow landing at one end. The landing was cold and perilous. Even in summer a winter wind would streak out from under doors to cut you about the ankles—and wrists if you happened to be, as Tots was, on all fours. For Tots could not bear the sensation, far less the certain knowledge, that the floor was swaying beneath her. The dilapidation in this part of the House was so far advanced that the landing was now strung between opposite ends like an interior suspension bridge. Defying all the laws of physics the rooms here hung together, resistance fighters against the decay, three on one side, three on the other and Mr. Hawkin's there at the end, two steps up.

Their doors hovered several inches above the worn boards, the gap between affording glimpses of the rooms below, here the top of a wardrobe piled with battered cricket gear and school hats, there the furred top edge of a downstairs door standing ajar.

Tots carefully straightened up. She opened the first of the doors and took a step into nothing.

The door squealed as it swung out over the room below with Tots pedalling air as she clung in mute terror to its handle. But Gordon, seated at the grand piano down below and intent on perfecting his own rendering of *There Is A Balm In Gilead*—by which means he hoped to insinuate himself still further in his father's favour—did not even look up.

The vast and lofty room over which Tots dangled like an unhappy angel was commonly known as the ballroom and was rarely used, on account of its floor's steep gradient. To hold a ball in this ballroom would have been to court accident and injury not to mention financial disaster for the Master (who knew the cost of personal liability). Guests who took to the floor would have found themselves listing dangerously long before the first drink had taken effect; even the piano, a most solid Bechstein, remained in place only by virtue of a wedge under one wheel.

Tots had often wondered about the two doors high in the wall; she was sorry she had found out. With agonizing slowness and with vigorous assistance from her skinny legs, which pumped back and forth for dear life, the door swung to again and Tots stepped back onto the landing.

"Well," she said, yanking at the sweater that had ridden up to her armpits, "that was a experience. Somethin' of a flyin' visit, you might say." Not wishing to repeat the thrill, Tots did not open the next door, knowing where it would lead her, but crossed instead to the one opposite. Inured now to the lesser perils of the landing, she was content to walk—but she held tight to the door jamb as she opened the door. It was the old bathroom, no longer used since the water heater, like one of the old space shuttles, had blown through the roof during the Solid Winter. A piece of orange plastic covered the hole but despite the new ventilation the room still smelled pissy. The moisture of two foggy centuries of baths had seeped into the very bricks and no amount of global warming would dry them out. The wallpaper hung in limp tatters and lichen patterned the walls in its place. Across the bare floorboards irregular tidemarks of verdigris and black concentred on a huge cast-iron tub, its clawed feet sunk deep in the spongy wood. Tots could not remember who slept in the room below.

Since there was no hiding place here for documents of any kind, it did not take Tots long to finish. She swept dutifully but nervously, treading with care and listening to the boards complain as a skater listens to thin ice. Her broom picked up blackened rolls of sticky dust and left ugly tracks across the floor so that it looked worse than when she started. But Tots was no perfectionist. She decided against even going into the next room where the floor sloped dangerously away to a hole in the far corner that showed the remains of a Turkish rug at its rim.

Tots did not like the look of it at all and besides there was nothing to search; either the hole had over time swallowed the contents, or the Master had had the room cleared to avoid that eventuality. In either case, Tots herself had no wish to disappear like laundry down a chute and she firmly closed the door.

The last room on this side, stacked with boxes three or four high and two deep around the walls, looked more promising but Tots soon realized that she was wasting her time for they contained nothing more than someone's short-sighted investment: eyeglasses and combs and toothbrushes still in their crackly packets. She crossed over. Her hopes that the contents of the other rooms might have been removed to this last came to nothing. The room was empty and very cold, but at least it looked reasonably solid. She began to sweep.

The bare boards reappeared like hanks of long dark hair in a cloudy river. When the floor was swept clean she rested. The sun was striking the light fixture in the centre of the flaky ceiling and the reflection from its droplets of glass lay like spilled water on the dark wood.

And then Tots remembered.

A cold winter, the coldest yet. And then another spring without sunshine. A summer spent pining for warmth, waiting. Working in hat and mittens. The dust falling from the sky like snow and no one to say where it was still coming from, this seven-year plague. All the family in overcoats and scarves, waiting. Still waiting for the market to recover. The Master angry, and most of all with Tots. And she sent to sweep in a far away room where the dry cold stuff sifted in around the windows and through the cracks under the sills. Sifted in and sifted in and she sent to sweep and no end to its drifting. Immaculate dust piling in corners in crescent dunes. Her breath condensing and freezing on the unlit glass of the chandelier, condensing and freezing so that the crystals of glass grew crystals of ice that tinkled distantly until Mrs. Phelum opened the door with a bang and the icy tears crashed on the swept floor.

"Gawd almighty! I been lookin' for you all over. How long you been up here?"

Tots shook her head.

"Who sent you?"

"Him."

"Why?"

"'Coz."

"What you done, then?"

"Nothin'."

"Well you must have done something. What?"

"I dunno."

"Well you said something, then."

"I never even seen him. I sent him a birthday card."

"Oh yes? You don't know how to write."

"Scoria showed me. She showed me what to put."

"And I suppose it was Scoria's idea, an' all?"

Tots nodded.

"So what did she tell you to write?"

"'Happy Birthday'."

"Oh yes?" Mrs. Phelum folded her arms. "But I don't suppose you could still write it, could you—'Happy Birthday'—if you was to be asked, I mean?"

"Yes I could. Me and Scoria writ it over an' over before I done it on the card, so's the letters would look nice."

Then Tots had gone over to the corner of the room. She had taken her broom and swirled the pile of snowdust she had swept. She had knelt and traced with her finger. Now, remembering, she could still see the pattern of the two words:

WHOISMY   MOTHER?

"See," said Tots, drawing her finger through the air under the words as she had seen Scoria do. "*Happy Birthday*. Then I put me name. Two trees, a pond, an a snake. Like she showed me: Tots."

Mrs. Phelum had taken the broom angrily and erased the letters in a blizzard. "Do yourself a favour, ducks," she said. "Don't send no more birthday cards." Tots closed the door quietly just as Mrs. Phelum had done all those years ago. The hand on her shoulder startled her so that a small shock wave rippled along the landing.

"Oh, Mr. Hawkin. I thought you was out."

Mr. Hawkin adjusted his glasses and looked around. "Well I am. I suppose."

Elderly and gentle, Albert Hawkin had the air of a patient sheep, with none of the sheep's rudeness. Mr. Hawkin, for instance, would never stare.

"No, I mean 'out'. You know."

"Oh, I don't go out much any more. I don't have time." He blew three short blasts of amusement down his nose and the landing responded with three short shudders. Mr. Hawkin collected clocks. "But what about you, young lady? You don't get up here too often."

Something about Mr. Hawkin invited utter honesty and Tots, like others, found herself telling the whole truth where half would have done.

"I'm lookin' for somethin'," she said.

"Tt-tt-tt. Just like the rest of them, all looking. Poking about their whole lives. Scraping and scrabbling. But if you asked them what they were looking for, could they tell you?"

He drew a deep breath and it was obvious that he was prepared to answer his own question, at great length.

"I can," Tots said quickly. "I'm lookin' for the rest of me indentures."

"Ah, I see," said Mr. Hawkin, meticulous still, showing no surprise. "And do you need them for any particular reason?"

"Personal."

He nodded once. "Ah," he said again, to indicate that it was all perfectly clear and there was nothing at all wanting in Tots's answer and silly of him really to have asked.

"I want to know me name for starters." The honesty, the openness of human beings was a constant source of delight to Mr. Hawkin.

"You could look on your birth certificate," he offered helpfully and then, seeing her sharp ferrety look, "or perhaps not. They might only show numbers now. I'm not sure. Look, it's chilly out here. Shall we go in?" He put his arm round her shoulder and helped her over the sloping floor and up the steps to his door.

Tots glanced up at him as they went in. It was usually Mr. Hawkin who was being led. Tots had seen him once crossing the road, Mrs. Pinnacle leading him by the elbow. She had always assumed his stairs didn't go all the way to the top.

As they stepped into his room the ticking settled about their shoulders and ears like locusts. Mr. Hawkin was evidently deaf to it; Tots was deaf to anything else. Tick-tick-tock-tock, tick-tick-tock. Hundreds of midget clog dancers running for their lives. Two steps forward, two steps back. Getting nowhere. Above it all was a slow, loud tick, heavy and wooden, a door to an empty room opening and slamming shut, opening and slamming shut. Mr. Hawkin smiled and mouthed to her. "Cup of tea?"

"Please."

He filled his kettle from a wash basin in the corner of the room and set it to boil on a rusty primus stove.

There were clocks on every wall, on every shelf and ledge, on the table and on the floor. Most of them were old; they had come from ships, from schools, carriages, from the façades of banks and the mantles of peers. But winking tartily between them were the shameless, insistent digitals, not watching politely, attentively until you wanted to know the time but telling you, telling you, whether you wanted to know or not.

"What's that?" Tots pointed to a small brightly lit display terminal. An unnatural whiteness blazed from its screen.

"That?" said Mr. Hawkin. "Just a clock."

"Don't look like one to me."

"No it doesn't much. It registers nanoseconds—billionths of a second—but of course our eyes can't apprehend the changing numerals, they come and go so fast."

"You mean there's numbers on there." Tots liked numbers; their agility pleased her.

"Oh yes. It runs on 'sputes'. They're the energy particles that fly off from the earth's spinning. It's constantly telling the time." Who to, wondered Tots, if no one could see it? Itself?

"How do you know," she said, "if you can't see the numbers?"

"Well you don't ever really know. No one does. It's beyond us. We just have to accept. And believe."

"Well I'd want to know if it was working at least."

"Oh it's working. We'll know if it ever stops because then the time will be fixed on the screen. At whatever time it stops, do you see? But of course then it will be too late."

Tots didn't think she wanted to ask the obvious question. Mr. Hawkin seemed to be suggesting the possibility of another mishap, one of even greater proportions.

She moved on until she came to a mechanical clock which stood on the floor and was constructed like a small tower. The tower housed two spirals which formed a twin staircase on which twelve men were stationed. At the top was a bell. The men worked their way up the ascending spiral. Every hour a new man would reach the bell, strike it the appropriate number of times and enter the twin spiral for his descent. At least you could see what they were up to.

"My little pastime," said Mr. Hawkin, watching her, and blew his three short blasts again. "Passes the time. Time passes, oh yes. But it's always with you. Now there's a conundrum has never occurred to you, I shouldn't wonder. If it passes where does it go? Can't go on ahead of us, can it? You'd have the past in the future. It's coming at us, isn't it? We're eating it up as we go, just to save ourselves from being run over. Until we can't eat fast enough. Think about it. It explains a lot."

He took a crazed brown teapot down from a row of clocks and warmed it from the kettle.

"But as I said, it's a pastime. Some people used to collect works of art. There were people who collected butterflies, stamps, first editions (I collect seconds)," there was no stopping him, his nose was a wind tunnel, "fine wines, rare coins, dust, debts. People collect their thoughts, collect their senses, excuse me while I collect myself—" Helpless, he gestured the wooden-faced Tots to a wooden chair.

She sat down while he made the tea and placed the pot between two mugs on a table.

"No, I'm saving time, really. That's what I'm doing. Most of these pieces had run themselves to a standstill at one time or another. I've just dusted them off and put them back into working order. Given them more time so to speak. But they fritter it. Listen to them. Racing away."

"Like they got no time to lose."

"Oh, very good, yes. Will you be mother?"

Tots took the heavy pot with both hands and poured out the strong red tea, drawing the pot up and down as Mrs. Phelum always did.

Mr. Hawkin watched her, smiling equably, his mind, which otherwise tended to run on like a decapitated chicken, soothed by the rilling of the tea.

"So I was looking for my indentures." It seemed necessary to prompt.

"Ah, yes. We were forgetting." He adjusted his glasses and straightened his face. "Where did you say you lost them?"

"I didn't. I only ever had one bit, see. *He's* got the rest."

"Ah, I see. It is in point of fact the Master's side of the contract we are looking for."

"Right."

"Have you ventured to ask him for it? Asked if you could see it perhaps? Take a little look?"

"You jokin'?"

"No. Quite. Well, is it absolutely necessary for you—"

The ferrety look returned, sidelong this time and Mr. Hawkin abandoned that particular line. "Why don't you just tell me," he said, "why you want to find this document so badly?"

"Well—don't tell no one? Promise?" Tots leaned over her mug of tea as she spoke, elbows wide as if to keep out potential eavesdroppers. "I want to run away."

"Then why don't you?" Mr. Hawkin was unshockable. "Just pack your suitcase and go. A moonlight flit." He was carried off into the vernacular by the sheer drama. "Why not?"

"Well, I gotta know what me name is first."

"You know what your name is. Tots!" He raised his mug to her, slopping his tea. "It's a good name."

"Yeah. Tots what? Tots zip. I ain't even got a mother. Nor a father. How would you like it?"

Mr. Hawkin could only smile sadly.

"I can't leave without knowin'. I can't just go out there an' make out I come from nowhere, can I?"

"Why not?"

"Because everybody comes from somewhere."

"Perhaps you didn't."

The thought had occurred to her. Hearing it articulated however was another matter. It was like being hit in the chest. "Don't be daft," she said.

Mr. Hawkin was not offended. "I'm serious. You have to contemplate that possibility, my dear. Perhaps you didn't. You might be wasting your time."

"No, you don't understand. I got to have them papers. Ben said. He said if I run away an' leave them papers behind, the Master'd get me. He'd come an' get me an' use them papers to prove I'm one of his belongin's. He said the Master'd stick it to me good and proper."

"That doesn't sound like Ben."

"Well, no. What he said was that it'd be all the worse for me if I got caught. He said get out but get them papers first. An' get rid of them. Then you can be your own master. Course he meant mistress."

"Well, I suppose he might have a point. The Master's sort never like to lose anything, however much they may have to start with. But it does seem like a great deal of bother—"

"I don't mind."

"—and quite likely to get you into a great deal of trouble if you're caught snooping about like this. What makes you so sure you want to run away, anyway? Things have changed out there, they tell me. Gone to pieces, so to speak, from what I hear."

"I don't care. Least there wouldn't be anyone tellin' me what to do all the time. I've had enough of this place, anyway. Ain't no one here cares about me. It's nothin' but work. I sweep till the broom's wore out an there's always more. The dust just keeps on goin' round. It gets picked up when the wind blows—you know what it's like—an' dropped every time the wind drops. Then there's all that filth they kick up just tryin' to keep this place standin', shorin' up walls here, knockin' 'em down there. I never get no rest. When they can't think what to do with me next they put me up the chimneys to sweep. I thought that sort of thing went out with donkey travel. It's criminal. You can't see for the dark an' you can't breathe for the soot an' all you can think of is gettin' out."

Mr. Hawkin averted his face. It was good that this flash flood of self-pity was happening in the privacy of his room, away from the others.

"Then there's Scoria. She's as spiteful as a rusty saw. An' now she thinks I'm goin' to do her work an' all. She thinks she's got me. And Gordon. He's another spiteful one. When he sees me comin' he kicks over a bucket of peelin's or summink, accidental like. He's into all kinds of nasty stuff, too. His pockets are always full of animal parts. But you don't want to hear about that."

"No, don't tell me what Gordon does. He came up here once without my knowing and attached a chicken's head to the cuckoo in that clock over there. I shall never forget. It was six o'clock."

"Or six o'cluck," said Tots, who would have liked to take the edge off the unpleasantness.

"No," Mr. Hawkin went on, "Gordon's a bad lot. Nothing would surprise me. Mrs. Phelum was just telling me—Mrs. Phelum, now, she's all right."

"Oh, Mrs. Phelum, yes. But she's always too busy. She don't take much notice of me."

"Well there's Ben."

"Yeah. Ben's all right. But he's got his rabbit, that one with the five legs what he found down the tracks last year. And his rat—until it disappeared. I asked him once who would he save if there was a fire: Dora the angora, me or the blind rat? 'Easy,' he said. 'Dora'd be outside already, I'm just his friend, so it'd have to be the rat. I'd have to save Faceful,' he said. 'She can't see. I couldn't let her burn.'"

Mr. Hawkin sighed for her pain. "This isn't getting us anywhere, is it? And I don't really know how to advise you. If you won't go to the Master you could go and see the Mistress."

"I did."

"Well go and see her again. Although I think if you really are going to run away, your best plan would be to stay out of trouble until then. Forget about these indentures and what Ben said and never mind what I said about a birth certificate. It may not after all exist, as I said before."

"What do you mean? I come from somewhere, don't I?"

"And if you don't? Would it make any difference? Really?"

Tots didn't answer.

"If you just are? These clocks, now. Somebody made each one of them. But not the time they run on. They make their own time. Does it exist without the clocks? Now supposing in your case time is the organism."

"That was really nice tea," said Tots quickly. The man's a fruit-cake, she said to herself. He's one short. They all told me he was. Poor old bloke. "Well. I'd best be pushin' off now," she said, mustering her manners. "It's been nice talkin'. Bye-bye."

"Just as we were getting somewhere." The ebb and flow of sadness was not to be resisted. "Good-bye, my dear. Perhaps we'll have more time next time."

The Woman in Silk

T ots made her way down as quickly as she could. Halfway along the middle landing she heard Uncle George at the door of the maids' parlour, or at least she heard Sherilee squeal and then she heard Morgan-The-Not-Very-Fey tell him to fuck off. Tots stepped back into an alcove and waited for him to continue in his restless quest for fresh flesh.

Morgan and Sherilee would be settling down to their cup of tea, a ritual that would have surely driven Morgan to drink had she not lobbied for a private maids' parlour for that very purpose. Three or preferably four shots of scotch in half a cup of Tetley's usually did the trick. She called it nettle tea for its sting.

Tots heard the front door being unlocked and then it slammed. That would be the thwarted Uncle George, taking himself out no doubt for an afternoon leer. Tots decided there and then to give Uncle George's room a quick once over. She went back along the landing and listened at his door to make sure he really had gone out. Once, several years ago, she had had an untoward surprise in Uncle George's room. "Funny," Mrs. Phelum had said, reading out the order and seeing that a new one had been scribbled in under the last. "Someone's added that bit. Wonder who writ that?" And Tots had gone to sweep.

She had knocked at the door and listened. "Come in!" George was always cheerful, always welcoming. Tots was halfway across the room before she really saw. He was sitting in a chair with his trousers round his ankles and something in his lap.

"Oh," she had said and had begun instinctively to back out.

"No, no, no. Don't go. Come in. Sit down." And he had patted it.

But Tots had somehow known to get out fast, and did. She had hurried away and sat on the stairs, her fingernails between her teeth. She was deeply puzzled until she realized his affliction. For at least a year after that she had a new respect for Uncle George: to be able to get about like other people, to remain so cheery, so uncomplaining. With the thing upside down like that.

She looked round the door. No nasty surprises. But paper everywhere. He had had his plans out again. He was working on a portable nuclear missle and had spread them over a pile of rubble in the corner by the window. No one believed he would get very far, assuming intelligence to be a prerequisite for success in the project. Morgan had said that was a rash assumption. She said idiots everywhere had been making them for years.

George's desk was awash with papers. There was nothing for it but to look through the desk and drawers item by item in search of the missing half. In the event and without reading, it did not take long and Tots came upon only two papers that had been torn; one was a photograph torn down its length and divorcing the beaming George from some female form whose thigh rested under his left hand; the other was a handwritten letter torn into confetti-sized pieces that she found in an old envelope. She knew it was old because the stamp bore the picture of a queen.

A glance under the bed confirmed that there was nothing there apart from the magazine stacks. It was where George kept his supply of men and women in poses as silly as those of the pets on Mrs. Phelum's calendar. There were two large ammunition boxes at the foot of the bed, filled, as George had once proudly explained, with the finest collection, of World War II hand-to-hand combat weapons to be found anywhere in London. He had promised Gordon the whole collection, to be handed over on his twelfth birthday.

"Nuvver good reason for goin'," reflected Tots as she closed the door.

She continued down to the Mistress's apartments and stopped opposite the door. She could hear the distant muted squawking of the baby. There was always a baby. It was only recently that Tots had begun to wonder how Mrs. Pinnacle concealed the bump each time and still more recently how she ever brought herself to do the thing Scoria had described in such ugly detail. The babies themselves were never seen. There was a wet nurse and of course there was a nursery and after that there would be the School of Access to teach the young how to access more than they already had, the same lessons in principle that children on the Outside were learning with a good deal more urgency.

Tots thought carefully about what Mr. Hawkin had said about the Outside. It wasn't that she was afraid of taking her chances out there; she would go today if she could. It was just that it wasn't much of a chance if the evidence of her indenture were still in the Master's hands. She would be like a mad yelping dog on the end of a retractable leash. Yoink. Back she would be at her master's trouser leg with a rolled up newspaper rapped smartly across the nose. No, a taste of freedom wouldn't be enough, not for Tots. She was ravenous. And besides there was Mr. Hawkin's proposition that she may not have come from anywhere. Tot was not afraid of very much, but there, like a mirror with no reflection, was an idea that gave her the creeps. Not come from anywhere? Belong to no one? That would be tantamount to reaching the park and finding yourself shut in forever. How long could you last rolling in the daisies and waving your paws to the clouds? No, she was not going to give up that easily. Mr. Hawkin was right about that at least: she didn't have to take no for an answer; there was nothing to stop her asking again. If she was serious about running away, what, seriously, could she lose? And there right opposite her was the door.

It was two o'clock in the afternoon, the day's counterweight to two in the morning when all the world hangs for a brief space in a state of suspended animation, a yo-yo at the bottom of a string.

Everything was quiet downstairs.

It was now or never. Tots began a quick rehearsal. Mrs. Pinnacle, she would say, I've had it. I'm up to here. I want to see them papers right now. I got the right. (She was pretty sure she hadn't but it was worth a try.) If you ain't got them who has? I don't mean to put you to no bother, like .... Now she was sounding too much like herself and was besides not sure how to finish. She threw away the script, crossed the landing and knocked on the door.

She knocked three times before very distantly she heard a voice reply. She went in and stood in the anteroom opposite a pair of large, carved doors. To her right the Mistress's bedroom door stood ajar. Powder blue was the signature in this room that Virginia Pinnacle liked to call her 'refuge'. Powder blue covered the bed, the mold on the walls; powder blue in a great swatch disguised the grime on the windows. And everything was padded: padded stool at the dressing table, padded chair at the desk at the swaddled window and padded headboard on the bed. Like for a lunatic, Tots always thought. On the bed an empty suit in smart cherry was laid out with its arms at twenty past eight. She must be in the nursery thought Tots. Tots had never been asked to enter the double doors to sweep but she had always assumed the nursery to be behind them. The doors were elaborately carved with birds and beasts of every kind. Snakes crawled up the edges of each panel and two of them rose to strangle the doorknobs. There were elephants and bulls, the sun and the moon, bears suckling their cubs and a she-wolf with dugs like icing bags. The voice came again.

"Come!" it called, throaty with sleep, and Tots went in.

In the centre of the room, under a canopy of Indian silk and reclining on vast billows of dusty velvet was ... not the Mistress. Not, at least, the coiffed and buffed, slicked, primped and powdered, deodorized, electrolysed Mrs. Pinnacle that Tots knew. This woman was dressed in some fluid kind of embroidered robe. Her hair coiled thickly at the base of her neck; it shone darkly in the densest places but was bleached to corn-silk on the top and streaked with strands of grey. By no stretch of the imagination could it be said to be 'done', only temporarily restrained. This was not the Mrs. Pinnacle who sent directives to the kitchen, who daily sallied forth to abuse and degrade all who were engaged in her service and many who were not. No, this was like no one Tots had ever seen in the house before.

Her skin was the colour of the pale Jersey cow but it looked creamy rather than velvety to touch and, oh, Tots wanted to touch, there was so much of it—the shoulders the neck, the full breast she was offering to the tiny wrinkled baby. It was an undulating, silky meadow of warmth, this skin; Mrs. Pinnacle, Tots had always thought, was covered in something like overstretched pastry. And the face! It bore as much resemblance to Mrs. Pinnacle's as a palomino mare's to a vole's. It was broad and flat and beautiful and no amount of man-hours at the salon would ever tailor this face to Mrs. Pinnacle's standards—ah, but it was lovely. It beamed loveliness, radiated it. The face of the mother of Saturday's child, loving and giving. Powerful, it had nothing at all to do with domination, everything to do with strength and protection.

The woman sat up, drawing her legs into an easy lotus so that the folds of her foreign-looking shift lapped behind her brown shins. Mrs. Pinnacle would do herself a mischief with her high heels, thought Tots. But if this woman was clearly not Mrs. Pinnacle, she was just as clearly no ordinary domestic and so who—on earth—was she?

"You can come and sit down," said the woman, patting the green velvet. "Please." And Tots could hear the word, a tender, succulent fruit in her mouth.

She went and sat down beside her, at first adopting the woman's pose and then, seeing that her own thin legs looked too much like the crossed bones of Gordon's poison collection, kneeling instead and sitting back on her heels.

The woman was very patient.

"So. He was lying. I knew he was. And you have finally come to see me. What a long time!"

"Oh—yeah. Is it?" Tots would have been grateful for more clues.

"Oh a lifetime. For you."

Tots laughed uneasily. "I suppose so."

The woman heaved a sigh of fierce, greedy satisfaction, making the baby squeeze its eyelids together all the more tightly. "But you're here. So now tell me what you want."

"Well, er, Mrs. ... um ..." Who was this woman?

"No, no, no. You call me Cali. It is my name."

"Well, er ... Carly, I'm lookin for somethin'. An' Mr. Hawkin—you know Mr. Hawkin?" It seemed only sensible to ask. "Well, he said like I should ask the Mistress."

"Yes?"

"'Coz I'm lookin' for me indentures. An' me birth certificate."

"What on earth for?"

"Well, everybody's got one, ain't they? An' I thought maybe I ought to check up on mine, seein' as I ain't never even seen it. I mean I don't even know who me mother is. Nor me father, come to that."

"Peugh! Father!" The woman shifted her baby to the other breast already squirting milky indignation at the mere mention of paternity. "You mean to tell me you don't know who your mother is?" She had her hand clamped over her left breast in an attempt to stem the milk which continued to flow and was now trickling through her fingers. Tots noticed for the first time a circlet of tiny bones around the woman's neck. And something began to stir in her consciousness, something triggered by the necklace of bones, or was it by the sight of the milk? She had an inkling that she could not quite suppress, one that she knew was about to blossom in her darkest ignorance like a giant firework.

"To be truthful," she said untruthfully—yet she had to lie for how could she even contemplate such a thing, far less say it—"no."

The woman smiled a sad, closed-lipped smile that was all beauty, all love. She put her palm on the baby's dark hair and stroked it, cupping her palm to its skull, caressing. Oh, the tenderness, oh, gentleness! O love—! Tots thought her heart would burst.

"You are!" she blurted. "You're me mum!"

The woman looked up and, tilting her head back, drew a deep breath, closing her eyes and snuffing up her satisfaction as if she could not fill her lungs enough, as if it were the scent of new-mown hay. Then, softly, slowly, and still smiling, she exhaled.

"I knew you would come," she said. "You must be Tots, my twenty-seventh born."

"Then—?"

"Yes. This—" she thumbed the baby's downy brow, "this is your little brother."

The baby stopped its sucking and looked up frowning under its mother's touch.

"Oh, he's sweet, inne?" said Tots obligingly. But there were too many questions and some of them were worrying.

"But if I'm your twenty-seventh...what about the other twenty six?"

"What about them?"

"Where are they?"

"Oh, here and there. There and here. Life is a cycle. We come, we go."

It was not a very satisfactory answer but Tots was not sure she was ready to press the matter. Still awed by the earthy beauty of the woman, she preferred for now to accept.

"Fancy," said Tots, happy. It wasn't at all how she had imagined her family, or her mother. She had pictured someone rather like a cross between Scoria and Mrs. Phelum, frazzled but with a heart of gold. It hadn't been a perfect picture but it had been one she could comprehend—and it would have done.

"There's Ben and Gordon too, of course." Ben and Gordon? What was she saying? All the circuits in Tots's brain were live and ready for input. She couldn't possibly mean what Tots thought she meant.

"You mean Mrs. Pinnacle—"

"Mrs. Pinnacle doesn't exist. She is a shadow, an illusion, a phantasm. She is a chimera. Mrs. Pinnacle is the dream you have after eating a banana at bedtime."

"You mean—"

"I mean—you're surely not dense, are you? You don't look it—I mean we are all one. One family. The world is my child."

Tots had no difficulty accepting this statement, given the woman's—her mother's—exorbitant style. It was a great fluffy cloudbank of extravagance and Tots climbed on. But she did not forget to take her baggage with her.

"So who's me father?"

Tots's mother looked at her and there was a glint of something hard in her glance, no more than a glint, a razor blade in the apple—but unmistakable. And then it was gone. "Why do you ask?"

"'Coz it's not Mr. Pinnacle, that's one thing. I know I ain't too bright but I ain't stupid neither."

Cali prised the baby, who appeared to have drowned in excess, from her breast and laid it gently on a pillow. Then, adjusting her kaftan, she got up and took Tots by the hand.

"Look," she said and led her to an alcove. Above three lighted candles stood a statue. Around its base, the playful figures of infants cavorted in a circle of endless innocence. Above them, her flat feet negligent in a tangle of silver offerings, squatted a broadhipped woman. Her left hand supported the head of an infant at her breast, its mouth latched tight to her nipple. Her own head was bent but she was not watching the suckling child. She was busy with her right hand lifting an infant by the arm, raising it to her lips. And her teeth were bared above its neck.

"Look. She creates all life. Do these children need a father?"

Tots couldn't help thinking that they certainly could do with a mother.

"All life. She gives birth to all and she consumes all. There is nothing else you need to know."

"What'll happen to him?" Tots pointed back to the sleeping baby.

"The same that happens to all. We live and we die. That is the whole story."

There was a stirring among the cushions, a faint sound. Again Tots was overwhelmed with this sudden rush of family.

"I'll have to tell Ben an' Gordon I know" she began. "Why didn't they tell me?" But her last word tailed away as the answer dawned on her. "They don't know, do they? They don't know you."

"In their hearts."

"Well, they'll have to be told. I'll have to tell them the truth. It's only right." But even as she was speaking she knew it wouldn't work. Not for a moment did she doubt any single word or syllable of what this woman had to say. But would anyone believe her, Tots?

"It won't work will it?"

The woman was serenely sad. "No one will believe you. And the Master—oh the Master would be very cross."

At these words, the enormity of her intention came home to Tots. To reveal the most private business of the Master, the innermost workings of his household, to point a finger at the heart .... Not to mention the private parts.

"Yes," she said, "I suppose he would." Tots left the Mistress reclining again with her milky baby. Her feet felt unsteady under the weight of the impossible knowledge.

Me mother! she said. But still it was hard to fathom and so, for all its glory, more than a little unsatisfactory. She may have found a mother to outmother all others, but the advantages as far as she could see were questionable. It was as if the woman, situated as she was at the very well-spring, had eyes only for the small fry that played in the emerging water; anyone, like Tots, about to go over the edge into the great, turbid river of life was beyond her range of vision. Why hadn't this mother of hers sought her out before? She obviously hadn't needed her. Wanted her? Even her own brothers didn't know her. And why, while she was on the subject, did they enjoy all the freedom and privileges of the House while she, Tots, was relegated, banished you might say, to the lowliest of positions?

But, come to think of it, was she, Tots, really ready to own them? Oh Ben, yes, but then he had been as good as a brother all along— better, she might even say, from her observations of brotherhood in action. Now, however, if she was truly related to Ben by blood, then equally she must be tied to Gordon. It was not a cause for celebration. How often had she pitied Ben his life in such close proximity to Gordon and his poisonous mind. It was no wonder to her that Ben should be up early each morning, pulling on his clothes as he headed for the door long before Gordon's first fart buzzed the fetid air of their room. No one, not even a nine-year-old boy could put up with the septic stream of sneering innuendo and the sudden threshing attacks of furious jealousy to which Gordon was prone. It would be like living in a swamp full of alligators.

And then of course there was the biggest alligator of them all. In his alligator shoes. Their aggressively shiny black. Coming at her with their snapping tread, down staircases and along hallways so that she must dodge into alcoves, doorways. It made her hair stand on end. The sadistically creased pinstripes scissoring, scissoring. He never saw her of course, his eyes being always firmly fixed on the prospect of profit.

It was easy to see where Gordon acquired his charms, sad that Ben should be saddled with such a pedigree, but impossible that she, Tots ... a tadpole .... She might as plausibly have spawned spontaneously in the mud of the Nile. But if not the Master, then who? It was all very well for the woman in silk to scoff but Tots knew better. No, of course it was not the Master; that was out of the question—but the question remained.

The Coal Shed

T he door to the twins' room was closed. Tots stopped and listened. Ben was not there. She could hear Gordon. Not sneering but simpering. He was talking to himself, practising his lines in front of the mirror. She could make out only some of the words: *Father, Please.* He liked to rehearse. She had seen him once before: *Father, Ben didn't mean to. It just slipped out of his hands.* Breaking wind as if for sound effects. Licking his palms to slick down his hair and try again. He was trouble even when you avoided him, his jealousy like a great uneven yoke across his back, the two buckets he must carry forever, forever unequal; Ben's buoyant, overflowing with the featherweight of imagined favour, his own containing nothing but a solid lump of imagined injustice, leaden.

Mrs. Phelum said it was all to do with the birth. Couldn't expect a body to behave normal after that. Longest nine months on record. Or something. Mrs. Phelum had delivered the twins herself, with difficulty. Gordon had been first and wouldn't come out. He was clutching onto something, she said. Didn't want to leave. Turned out it was Ben's ankle. Jealous right from the start, Gordon was, she said. Couldn't bear to think of Ben in there with it all to himself. Put his ankle all askew. Spiteful. Ben the dreamer, though, he was born sleeping.

And it was true. Unmoved by the violence of his arrival—except to shiver when they prised his brother's hand away—Ben had slept on for two days, dreaming, mouth foreshadowing a smile, only opening when he caught the scent of milk, until, on the third day, while Haggerty was doing some repair work, the back wall of the house had given way and he had woken to the crash, so surprised and amazed by blue that he lost what he was dreaming. It left him looking wistful. An endearing look. Gordon could have killed him for that look.

Tots went outside and found Haggerty in his shed, sawing.

"Seen Ben?"

He turned his face towards her and nodded.

"Where is he?"

Haggerty, still smiling, shook his head, raising his eyebrows to disclaim all cognizance of anything.

Know who I am? Tots was tempted to ask. But it would not have been any good. Haggerty was certain of only one thing—and that had to do with his own identity and was, according to everyone else, most likely mistaken. Everyone else was most likely right. Haggerty did not have much memory of his childhood. With a single, notable exception, Haggerty did not have much memory at all in the conventional sense. The inside of his head was a soundless, sightless space, and wordless. Before the Mishap his teachers had given him a label which did nothing to alter his condition but spurred his classmates to think of more catching ones, Baggy Brains Haggerty being one of the less savage. There was no commentary inside Haggerty's head, no text, however brief, to register or elucidate events. Haggerty never went so far even as to think: *starting to rain,* or, *the Clapham bus.* Life outside his head existed for his use but never intruded on the ample space within. If

Haggerty lay down and closed his eyes he saw no replays of the day's activities, not even Polaroid stills; he heard no echoes, was never, therefore, moved to laughter or to tears. Inside Haggerty there was only the sense of being, which hummed through him like a current of energy. Where others had sound and vision Haggerty 'had' sensations. He possessed them; he experienced them wholly. He never diluted them with interpretation. In fact Haggerty's memory was prodigious; it simply recorded life differently, was a different kind of camera. He could even remember his own birth: it felt as if he had been growing in a bamboo cage. He could not see the cage nor think of it, nor describe it as such, but that is how it felt, and the cage as he expanded had contracted in order to invert and thrust him out. It was as if a sweater made of tough, springy bands was turning in on itself to push him out through the neck, all of it accompanied by something to do with balloons and their shrinking suffocating suction on skin when their own skin contracts. The membranous tension across the face, the pressure of the bamboo cage inverting, inverting until it yielded and was gone, he felt it all. Yet Haggerty was no more capable of describing or interpreting the sensation in recollection than he had been at the time. He had no wish to. This experience and others would return fresh each time to be relived without his ever knowing what the sensation signified. In Haggerty's head there were only signifiers.

This condition was not without its problems. Sometimes his disdain for the signified would infect events outside his head; as the morning in late adolescence when he got up and looked in the mirror and saw only a splash of light. Eventually, like a positive image developing, his face appeared, the thin reddish beard, the hollow cheeks. Haggerty did not think, 'Me!' as others might have done, but only smiled in greeting.

The single exception to Haggerty's manner of processing his life was a childhood memory of his mother, or anyway the back of his mother. She was flying at a noisy little man who held a bottle of beer up by the neck like a rattle. This image spontaneously occurred from time to time in technicolour with perfect resolution and lifelike movement but accompanied by a poor soundtrack distorted by his two-year-old screams.

For years he did not know its meaning until the day, abandoned by those who had classified his case as hopeless, he saw Mrs. Phelum on Platform 4 of the Northern line at Kings' Cross. And she was in full flight. He was sitting at the bottom of the steps with his paper cup of change, not too far from the spot where three young men were energetically engaged in assailing a fourth. Mrs. Phelum could not stand bullying. She achieved lift-off a split second before her body made contact with the young man with the bottle. Struck by what he thought had been a train, the young man had nothing to say for himself. His body slammed against the wall, still vertical but feeling as if it had fallen from a twelfth-storey window. Mrs. Phelum, rolling against him, turned to review the situation on the platform. The other two attackers were fleeing towards the exit at the other end. Their victim was running after them, glancing nervously behind.

Mrs. Phelum took her weight off the young man and said, "Well then,"

His colour began to return to normal.

"Well, go on, then. What you waitin' for? Christmas?"

He moved off warily, gradually gathering speed.

Mrs. Phelum bent to pick up her handbag and saw the other young man who had been begging on the steps. He was getting up and coming towards her with his arms outstretched.

"Mum!" he said. "Mum!"

"If you want change just ask for it like anyone else."

"It's me!"

She was rifling in her bag but it was hard to concentrate. The effects of the exertion were beginning to overtake her and her knees wobbled.

"It's me, Mum."

All she had in her purse was a five pound note and she needed it.

"Come on," she said. "A nice cup of tea."

It was the first of many. Whatever chord the young man struck in Mrs. Phelum's breast it resonated and reverberated for many years, carried him on waves of maternal need or guilt or love back to the dismal rooms she shared with her sister and on eventually to the big house in Pimlico. Mrs. Phelum and the young man seemed to be related, though no one was sure; if you asked Mrs. Phelum she would answer, in that tone, "Does it look like it?" And if you asked Haggerty he would turn his lean face to you, suck on his cheeks a bit and say, "I can't remember"—exactly as he did now when Tots asked him where he'd last seen Ben.

Tots found Ben outside in the coal shed, tending to Lilly. He was raking out the sawdust while Lilly lifted her hooves, panic rising in her great eyes as she considered the uncertain number of her legs. By the time Tots came upon him, her nerve had left her. Brother he might be, but he was also Ben, the Master's son—a decent little bloke, a good kid, but one of them all the same. Ben you're my brother! He wasn't going to believe her.

"Hallo, Ben."

"Hi."

"What's up?"

"Nothing."

"They put you to work?"

"Sort of."

She did not really want to know more. Not now. The new knowledge was like a face against glass, pressing.

"Ben—?"

"I suppose you want to know why?"

"Not right now. Ben ... ?"

"Because I beat Gordon up, that's why—"

"You know your Mum ...?"

"—the little jerk— What about her?"

"Do you know who she is?"

"What do you mean, 'Who she is?'"

"Who is she?"

"You know who she is."

"Well just say."

"Her name?"

"If you like."

"Virginia. Virginia Pinnacle."

"And she's your mother?"

"Yes."

"Are you sure?"

Now Ben stopped raking. "Tots ...."

But she was relentless. "How would you know? If she wasn't?"

He waited, patient.

"I mean what if she said she was."

"She never said she was."

"There you are then! She could be anybody. Ben—she might not be your real mother!"

The statement was a wild card; conversational conventions were

67

demolished. What could one say? Ben tucked in the extreme corners of his mouth, just slightly. It felt safest.

"Ben!" Tots pulled him by the upper arm; she might have had his ear. Lilly lowed with anxiety. "Ben I know who my mother is—she's the same as yours. Ben, it's Cali!"

"Oh, her!" Ben released himself. "That's the wet-nurse, stupid. Wet is the word."

"No, listen. She told me."

"Yes. She told me once."

Tots thought she had been prepared for any reaction, but this blasé dismissal had not figured.

"And Gordon. He said she was a witch."

"But you believed her?"

Ben thought it better not to answer.

"You mean to say you went in there and you saw her and you didn't feel nothing? Not anything?" Never had she felt her outlook more bleak.

"I think she says it to everyone."

Tots's dismay only deepened. She bit on her thumb.

"But we could pretend. I don't mind doing that. You be my sister; we have the same mother, but nobody knows; and there's this step-mother ...."

"Oh, save it," said Tots. "I don't want to play games. Save it for someone your own age. I'm off —" But she stopped, remembering. "What did you say about Gordon?"

"I beat him up."

"You did?"

"I had to."

"What'd he do to you, then?"

"Nothing. I did it for Faceful."

"I thought you lost Faceful."

"Gordon's got her."

"Where?"

"I don't know. That's why I beat him up. He said he's doing an experiment on her. With a jam jar."

"Oh, no. Come on. You don't have to believe everythin' he says." But she believed. She had seen it just the other day: one of Gordon's neatly labelled jam jars like a preserve from another age but with small holes pierced in the lid. It had been difficult to make out what was inside; whatever it was had pressed everywhere against the glass that was fogged and smeared. And then she had not wanted to see more, knowing that it was alive, and so when she loosened the lid to set it free she had turned her back and hurried from the room. It was a moment of cowardice and she had known it would haunt her.

"You know he's a liar," she said.

And then what Ben said next seemed to change everything. His voice was constricted with offence and indignation. "He's my brother!"

Tots looked at Ben to make sure he was serious, saw that he was, and braced herself for the door that slammed in her face. It wasn't quite what she had had in mind with respect to kinship and loyalty.

"Well, I'll leave it to you, then." That settled it. She would get those papers. And she knew what she would do with them now. She would destroy them. Then she would be off. No point in hanging around where you wasn't wanted.

The Cellar

"Cellar stairs," said Mrs. Phelum without turning round. Her knife was rocking over the mound of bloodied chicken liver with alarming speed.

"Cellar stairs?"

"What it says, ducks." Mrs. Phelum pointed the blade of her knife to the mammy's apron. "And while you're there you can make yourself useful and fetch a couple of crates of ginger ale."

"O.K.," said Tots, seeing new possibilities, and left once more for the broom cupboard.

Mrs. Phelum nicked the last small prism of liver neatly in two and scraped the mess into a bowl. It splashed a little.

"Nothing like it," she said and wiped her hands on her apron.

Mildred, chopping onions with infinite torpitude, cupped her hand to her mouth and gagged.

"Oh, pull yourself together," said Mrs. Phelum. "We've got a long ways to go yet. Now there's the tripe boiling over."

Mildred ran from the room as the lid of the pan rose on a cushion of brown foam.

Mrs. Phelum sighed mightily. Her kitchen looked like a ransacked cookhouse, cans and sacks of foodstuffs everywhere pillaged and abandoned, puddles of milk on the table and dollops of dough where they were least expected. With her sensibilities, Mrs. Phelum, elbow deep in abundance, might have been expected to spare a sigh for the hungry Outside, or, if not for them, then at least for the abundance itself, the excess of it, the waste of it. But the thought did not occur. You had to live. This was the way you lived. Who was she to say? And all that. And anyway, wasn't it the Master's doing? The Master amassed all the stuff in the first place, gathered it all unto his greedy bosom. It wasn't up to her kind to go round asking awkward questions. Given a choice between belly full, belly empty, not too many awkward questions occurred.

It was hardly surprising then that a certain wilful blindness in ethical matters prevailed. What was less explicable was that the most importunate question should be resolutely repressed: *what when?* What when it all runs out? Mrs. Phelum's sighs were for nothing so difficult. She sighed—contentedly—at the mountain of work before her, that was all. No one could say she was afraid of work. The table was dauntingly full of pies, pâté, jellies and a fruitcake, all in the making. But she'd get there. One step at a time. Three large hampers stood by already half full. Never say die.

Mildred, grey, reappeared. She held her hands limply at her breast as if they were two dead pigeons.

"Look. Pears," said Mrs. Phelum. "Now they don't make you queasy, do they? Get them cans open and drained darlin', and listen—get your skates on, will you?

"Scoria!" She raised her voice to an improbable pitch and Scoria came, cursing, with a wasp in her hair. She knocked it away.

"What?" In Scoria's mouth the word took on unprecedented overtones of bitterness and resentment.

"Get yourself in here and lend a hand. There's a pudding nearly ready and the pasties to be crimped and that duck wants pressing."

Mildred made a funny noise. Scoria did not reply. Her mouth was set like a drawer-pull as she looked Mrs. Phelum in the eye.

"*If* you don't mind," said Mrs. Phelum. *"Please."*

"Thank you." Scoria, satisfied, went over to the table.

"Hands!"

Scoria stopped. She pursed her lips, turned and scuffed back to the sink, where she held her hands briefly under a dribbling tap before drying them on an apron the colour of Mildred's face.

"I dunno," she said, "why we need all this stuff anyway. I can tell you now what'll happen."

"Just get on with it, will you. We don't need no telling."

"Her Ladyship, Mrs. Your Honour Pea-knuckle, won't touch a thing 'cause it's her bridge night and she gets wind. And Mr. Big, his Lordship, won't even come, that goes without saying. All of them crying babies'll be full of tit from that wet-nurse woman. Mr. Hawkin'll find a watch in the sand and take it apart. He won't have time to eat. Dear old Uncle George'll be busy getting a *feel* for the place. Ben'll—"

"Yes and you know everything, except how to press duck." Mrs. Phelum nudged her out of the way and began turning the handle with such force that Mildred had to suck in her cheeks and look the other way.

"There!"

"As I was saying—" Pointedly unimpressed, Scoria resumed her task.

"We know what you were saying. The Day Out's not for them, though, is it? No one expects them to sit round lookin' as if they're enjoying theirselves. Like us."

"—the Old Lady'll give all her food to that disgusting dog. Sherilee and Morgan'll hit the bottle. Jacky'll go looking for them addicks—"

"He said they were poets."

"—he met last year . Mildred'll be sick—oh, excuse me, I didn't see you there, you was so quiet. Tots'll be the only one wants to eat and he'll see she don't get the chance—"

"Or you will," Mrs. Phelum had had enough and said so. Her bulk was handy. She turned on Scoria and bulldozed her back where she belonged.

"And you and me'll be so sick of the sight of it all we won't want none." Scoria would strangle her grandmother for the last word and

Mrs. Phelum was about to tell her as much when the light at the top of the cellar stairs popped as Tots touched the switch.

Ever since the shut-down of the factories, the extinction of a single bulb was viewed in a new and dismal light. Its expiry was received with a particular kind of sinking dread and an uncomfortable hiatus always ensued while light bulbs that had gone before were remembered.

Tots walked her hand across a high ledge in the half dark at the top of the steps. Something in turn walked across her hand. Eight legs. Long as it wasn't a beetle. She found the matches and the candles. Replacement bulbs were kept under lock and key, possibly in the very place that documents were kept.

The cellar was not the ordered storage space it had once been. For many years it had been used largely as a tip, a roomy repository for all the lame inventions and limping wizardry of pre-Mishap life. Scoria threw bags of rubbish down too from time time. Items lay about at random among the rotting cabbage stalks and broken glass: a sunbed with a blackened pillow, an electric staple remover, a laser fly trap, an electric ice cream scoop, a gas-powered curling iron, a vacuum for autumn leaves, two knife sharpeners, three toasters, an answering machine and a fan. There were two computers, a printer, an electronic sewing machine, a food blender, a water softener, and two VCRs. Tots looked inside the microwave that had lain on its side down here for as long as she could remember with a risen cake still inside and the digitals stuck on "Done". She looked for mold. There was not any.

There was a box of books and Tots rummaged through hopefully but there were no papers. The shelves around the walls had not been disturbed for perhaps ninety years. They were filled mainly with preserves, some of which had grown furry hats with long threads trailing to the bottom of the jars. There were bottles of home-made wine, too, the reason for its continued existence clearly labelled: 'turnip'. Further along, the slatted shelves bore a strange harvest of bluish-roundish or longish-brownish, exhausted-looking things that expired in a puff at the touch of a finger.

Walking past the boiler room, Tots continued to the end wall with its red-painted door. This was where the Master had been excavating his personal shelter against Armageddon, expecting perhaps that it would come like a ton of bricks instead of in the way that it almost did, like a breath, under doors and down shirt collars, smoke from a distant fire .... He had lost interest then, finding his fears at the same time well-grounded and unfounded, himself saved. He settled instead for a front door. It was flanked by pillars and two stone urns from which skeletal geraniums craned, offering albino leaves to the dark.

Tots bent down and peered through the brass letter slot, holding the candle as best she could to see. There, right in front of her eyes ... she could just make it out in the partially excavated wall...it looked very like .... Her scalp tingled. She held the candle closer to shed more light through the slot. It was ... alight ... her hair was alight. She spat on her hands and the hair at the side of her head fizzed. All that remained was a patch of tiny frizzled hooks. Scoria would have a field day when she went up. But still she had seen it. There behind the locked door. She took one more look. A safe.

Sweeping the cellar stairs was nothing now that she had an objective and she finished quickly. She found the crates of ginger ale stacked up near a fleet of empty wine bottles and dusty carboys and with much blowing through clenched teeth she carried them up to the kitchen.

"There!' she said. "Anythin' else?"

"No—yes. You can pack them pies in. Get them out the way."

Scoria slopped by with a pail of grey water. "Movin' up in the world, eh?"

Tots chose to ignore. "The light's gone," she said to Mrs. Phelum. "I heard it."

"I suppose he keeps the spares in the safe."

"What safe?"

"The safe down there." Tots tilted her head towards the cellar.

"Aah!" Scoria screamed with delight. "Velcro head! What did you do? Stick your head in the oven?"

Mrs. Phelum glared at her until she went on outside with the water.

"You not seen it?" Tots persisted.

"No, ducks. You packing them in straight? The gravy'll be all over if they tip up."

"You haven't seen the front door, then?"

"Here, put these sandwiches down the side."

Tots was quiet for a moment watching Mildred picking the stalks of chicken feathers from a carcass.

"Well, there is a safe," she said.

"If there is it's not been used in years. Not for light bulbs and I don't suppose for money."

"Mr. Pinnacle doesn't need money," said Mildred. "Not when he owns everything there is to buy."

"Don't you be too sure about that. He's in trouble with his partners if you ask me. Has been for weeks." Mrs. Phelum hauled a leaden pudding out of the boiling water at the back of the hob and set it to cool. "That's why this place is up for sale."

"As if anyone could buy it."

"As if anyone'd want it."

"What if someone does?"

"What?"

"Want it. What'll happen to us?"

Mrs. Phelum thought. "Don't think no one's ever thought to ask," she said. "But he's not going to get rid of it, not in this state. It's all his. There's no one else can take it off him, much as he'd like. He's going to be left holdin' this baby for a long time. For good, if you ask me, but don't tell him that. Now get on. Back steps."

"I already done them."

"Garden path."

"He'll have me out on the street next."

"Tots!" Always swift to detect the stirrings of insubordination, Mrs. Phelum used a gently rising scale.

Tots sighed.

The Garden

T ots knew something was amiss when she saw the mermaid.
The path at the back of the House skirted the Mistress's enclosed courtyard and led away into the garden itself to the tawdry mock baroque of a concrete effigy, a chipped and flaking mermaid. Balancing on the tip of its tail in the centre of what should have been a fountain, it leaned precariously backwards and raised its arm in eternal, dull obedience to the artist's desire to convey languor. In the stubby hand that was poised above the statue's lumpy face, someone had wedged an upturned bottle of scotch. Tots climbed up and jiggled the bottle free.

Then her mouth was a fledgling's beak at the glass neck. But no drops remained. She contented herself with a sniff powerful enough to make her nose burn and contemplated her task.

The dirt on the path was dirt as only London dirt could be. There was more to it than weatherdust. It was the same dirt that compacted under the fingernails of waifs and weighed the trouser cuffs of the placeless: a silt rich in pulverized cement and brick dust, asbestos, lint, soot, coal, gravel, grit and tarmac, a silt that formed the perfect suspension for pink fibrefill, flakes of rust and shards of glass, iron filings, bobbles of polystyrene, bubbles of polythene, ground chalk, bone, china, and bits of ring-pulls. Dry as it was, this dirt did not fly up in airy clouds but massed itself into heavy dunes in front of the broom. The air all the same began to turn grey and the lining of Tots's nose began to prick and burn even more. Her lips smarted.

She stopped and surveyed her work. The path to the fountain showed clearly now between the grey nettles. She started on the path that led away through the jetsam of the House towards Haggerty's shed at the end. Ever conscientious, Tots followed with her broom where it led, past the broken lawn-chairs with their shredding nylon, past the rusted buckets perforated by thistles, the fuel cans bursting with dock, on under the collapsing arbour that had dropped its flakes of paint like creamy petals in the dirt, past the old car seat from from which the springs struggled, past the car itself, a red Honda without wheels or windows, past the dead—
"Oh, no," Tots dropped her broom and bent down to the cat. "Oh, you poor thing."

It was Roger the scrawny gay and he was stiff as a bedboard and reeked of whiskey. "Oh, you poor thing," Tots said again, stroking its bronze fur. She picked it up and looked down the path: a heap of plastic pipes, a rusty oven, and there she was, or there anyway, over the end of a turquoise bath tub and sticking out like a bowsprit, were Morgan's feet, slimly elegant—even in run black nylon—and dangling the familiar high-heeled court shoes from the toes.

"Oh Gawd," Tots said and hurried down the path. She had been expecting something of the sort but she had hoped at least to find the maid conscious. "What you doin' here?"

Morgan wetted her lips. It was going to be an effort.
"Murra."
"Pardon?"
"Murradah. It's murradah."

"What is?"

"Drinking. 'Smurradah drinking alone."

"It's murder for the cat," said Tots. "You've killed him."

Morgan opened her eyes long enough to have the sad news confirmed by the sight of the stiff Roger cradled in Tots's arms.

"Ach! Ma dearest friend. Ma ainly friend."

"You ought to have treated him better." Reproof was too tempting.

"I ainly wanted tae make him happy. I didnae want tae hurt him." Morgan sat up and used her apron on her nose.

"Oh, come on," said Tots, who though she was still cross, could not bear tears. "He probably never felt nothin'. Cheer up. We'll give him a nice burial then you best go and clean yourself up." She made off up the path and returned with a garden fork, of sorts. Morgan began to crank her long limbs out of the bath; she balanced her face unsteadily above them and meekly followed Tots through the grey weeds. The neglected earth had cemented hard but Tots would not be beaten. Though one tine was missing from the fork and another was doing the goose-step, she managed at last to break the ground.

Morgan swayed patiently as Tots negotiated the thistles to retrieve the curved iron door of an old stove; she used it to shovel away the dirt and stones and in this way made a respectable trough. It filled Morgan with a confusion of admiration and scorn; Morgan never did anything the hard way—but resourcefulness, that was something.

Tots laid the cat on the cradle of rusted iron and paused.

"Want to say somethin'?"

"I used him."

"No, I mean like a prayer or somethin'."

"Ach! Prayers! Who the hell has time for prayers when their ainly friend is dead and gone?"

"Well," Tots was hesitant now before the pain, "I just thought like it was the right thing. I mean people do."

"Aye," Morgan stared glumly at the corpse. "They do. What do you suppose they pray for? I've never been tae a funeral, I always send Sherilee."

"Well, um—for the, you know, deceased."

"Oh, I know that, but what for?"

"So's they get to heaven of course."

"Och, imagine! All of them. They're not all such guid friends as

Roger. If everyone prays for everyone else and they all get up tae heaven they'll all be there, waiting for us. It'll be just the same up there as it is down here. I'm going somewheer else when I go."

"I 'spect you are," said Tots. "But it'd still be nice for him. I think you owe it to him. A few words."

"Oh, all right." The smell of earth was helping her head no end. "We'll send him off. You lead and I'll follow."

Tots cleared her throat. "O Lord ..."

"I thought so."

"O Lord, for this here is a very fine cat ..."

"'Was'."

"Who never done no harm ..."

"Who did no harm ..."

"To nobody ..."

"Tae anybody ..."

"And never showed his claws ..."

"And never ...Wait a minute."

Morgan rooted in the pocket of her skirt and pulled out a packet of Players.

"Can't you wait till we're through? It don't seem right."

"Hold your noise." Morgan slipped two out and lit them one after the other. Then she broke a twig in half and using the pieces as holders stuck the cigarettes into the mound of earth, one on each side, smoking peacefully. Tots was happy with the effect.

"An' never bit ..."

"And did not bite ..."

"Who only wanted a good time ..."

"Who ainly wanted a guid time ..."

"An' never asked for nothing," especially not a drink, Tots was thinking, but kept it to herself, "'cept kindness ..."

"And asked for nothing except kindness ..."

"Who used to look real sharp ..."

"Can you no get tae the point?"

"We ask you Lord to make him happy ..."

"Where'er he be ..."

"Nor give him no cobwebs to lie on ..."

Morgan looked askance at Tots. She did not like to raise the issue of pertinence in the face of such fervour. She settled instead for "Amen."

"Amen," said Tots.

Morgan bent down and removed one of the cigarettes. She stuck it in her mouth. "There, Roger," she said. She had to close one eye against the smoke as she threw a handful of earth onto his side. "We'll say no more about it."

The two of them covered him up with dirt and executed a little fancy footwork to tamp it down. "That was nice," said Tots. "He'll appreciate that."

Morgan belched. "Debatable," she said. "But I did. Come on now. Time you got on with your path."

"An' time you got cleaned up. You smell like one of them carboys in the cellar. Maybe you could chew some weeds or somethin'."

Morgan looked up from the seam she was straightening. "You're all right, lass," she said. "If you're ever in trouble, you know where to come."

"Me? I'm in trouble now. Trouble's me middle—" But even as she spoke Tots heard trumpets, saw walls tremble. "Morgan—?" The clash of cymbals. Why hadn't she thought of it before? "Morgan? Didn't you tell me once you was in the slammer?"

"If I did I told you to forget it, too."

And the stones were toppling, tumbling now.

"No, but maybe you could help. I'm lookin' for some papers, see, and there's this safe ..."

"Who told you I was in for safe-breaking?"

No one had, but now the walls came crashing down. "You did," she lied. And the rubble lay all around. "You said you was real good at it. You said it was how you got your name, Morgan-The-Not-Very-Fey."

"Well, anyway?"

It was a relief to see that Morgan did not want to pursue the matter. "Well, anyway, I really need these papers, see, an' there's this safe down in the cellar ..."

"Oh no. I work here, girl, and I have no intention of applying for a permanent position elsewheer. Like Holloway."

"No one'd know. Mrs. Phelum said it ain't been used for years."

"There you are. Mrs. Phelum knows."

"But no one would know if you was to open it. No one ever goes down there. No one."

"What were you doing down there?"

"That's a silly question, innit?"

"Oh, yes. Poor little Cinderella. Sweeping the ashes of the day."

"No. Lookin' for me papers. Go on, help me. Please?"

"I'll think about it, lass. I'll think about it." She gave Tots's arm a quick squeeze before she teetered off up the path. Tots took up her broom and continued in the other direction, extemporizing on Roger's theme as she went.

"For he never complained and was patient. For he looked after himself an' never made no fuss. For he kept himself clean—about the only thing in this House that did—an' his breath never smelled, not like Belinda's. Oh, he was a lovely cat an' I hope he gets to heaven. It'd be all right with me. You wouldn't catch me complainin' if I got in an' he was there. See a friendly face. Should've thought that was the whole point."

She stopped before she reached the end of the path, her way blocked by a stack of buckled iron girders.

"Anyway, I would have thought anyone'd think theirselves lucky just to get in. If I was Morgan I wouldn't be so picky. She's pushin' her luck, that's what she's doin'. If there's Anyone listenin'."

The Parlour

Morgan's seams were still not straight. Nor was her cap. She rounded the mermaid at an angle, wobbling on her heels, an escapee from a French farce, were she less Amazonian; the villain in the pantomime since she was not. In flimsy disguise.

She reached the steps just as Sherilee opened the door.

"Oh, there you are!" The superfluous remark was Sherilee's special gift.

"Shit!" said Morgan as she missed the bottom step.

"Mind you don't fall."

Morgan briefly considered knocking Sherilee down.

"And hurry up, for goodness' sake."

"What for? Oh, don't tell me. If it's the Old Lady again I shall go back and have another bottle."

It was, of course. It was always the Old Lady. She was the parlour maids' cross which they bore with steadily diminishing patience, buoyed only by the reflection that Old Ladies are renowned for the sometimes providentially freakish nature of their bequests. She lived in the dusty parlour at the front of the house on the main floor and believed the maids to be entirely at her personal service because she chose to call this living room of hers the parlour. They were obliged to open the curtains for her, draw them closed. Then draw them back again. To lay a fire in the hearth, to light it, damp it. And lay another. There was nothing to stop them making her tea. Or perhaps she would have a cordial. She dropped her knitting needles down the back of her chair as often as she needed more butter for her toast. But never at the same time. Morgan had toyed with the idea of using the bell pull to pull the bell off the wall. But it was never wise to provoke Belinda.

Belinda was the Old Lady's noisome lapdog. It was less a dog than a loose agglomerate of bones assembled haphazardly in a sac of skin. The sac of skin was covered in sparse hair and running sores. No one other than the Old Lady had ever tested the commonly-held hypothesis that it would be nasty to pick up. Belinda kept most approaches at bay simply by breathing, for her mouth when it was open (and she could not breathe with it closed) reeked of tainted milk and blown meat and sported two needle sharp teeth, one upper, one lower, which she saved for innocent wrists or ankles. For feeding she depended on her mistress, who possessed a serviceable pair of dentures. Although they were somewhat loose, they did serve, if she chewed steadily throughout the day, to masticate considerable quantities of food in small portions. A visitor to the parlour at whatever hour of the day might find the Old Lady ruminating over a tough piece of gristle or a parson's nose. To have to wait for the morsel to reach the required degree of tenderness, knowing it would soon be removed and fed to the voracious Belinda, was psychological abuse in its most exquisite form.

"Come in," called the Old Lady. Deaf as a doorstop, she made it her custom to call 'Come in' at regular intervals to be sure that she kept no one waiting.

At the sight of the maids, Belinda jumped down from her mistress's lap and ran snapping towards them. Morgan growled very low and Belinda jumped back up.

"What can we do for you, Ma'am?" Morgan made no concessions to deafness. Her heavy accent thwarted all attempts to lip-read on the part of the Old Lady, who had long ago concluded that she was Spanish.

Sherilee was less callous; she rose to the challenge each time, saw herself perhaps reaching across deserts of wordlessness to make the first contact with an alien tribeswoman. "Uhwhat uhdo yoo waaant?" she asked. The vowels, distorted, hung from her adenoids, her mouth a gigantic echoing cave around each word.

"The fire, dears. Make up a nice fire, will you?"

"Dear God, it's August. Tell her it's August, Sherilee, for Christ's sake." Morgan's head was throbbing badly.

"Ihht's Aauughuust."

"Yes." The Old Lady laughed. "All dust. All dust and ashes. *'Tis all thou art and all the proud shall be.' 'Dust to Dust.'* Dust in our hair and ashes on our lips. Needs a good clean out."

"Not the only thing around here." Morgan was losing patience. "Look, Ma'am. If I may." She went over to the Old Lady's chair and, clenching her teeth in disgust, grasped Belinda by the scruff and deposited her on the hair-covered cushion of the other easy chair. Belinda, taken off guard, was too surprised to bite.

"Look, Ma'am." The maid put her arm behind the Old Lady's back and winkled her out of the chair, guiding her over to the window. Sunlight filtered in on them through the yellowed lace and the wings of bluebottles. "It's summer." With her free hand Morgan drew the curtain aside. The sun blazed in. The skin of the Old Lady's face was papery, delicate as the palm of a newborn. Outside, the street was thick with dust. It glittered. Two street children played on the railings in front of the boarded-up house across the street.

"It's summer, Old Lady."

"Tut! Summer already! Where the time goes! It'll be Christmas before you know it. Oh, the summers we had!" The Old Lady shook her head, rattling the empty deck chairs in the back of her brain. "The summers! And we knew how to enjoy them. We lived in the old house then. Had our own orchard. That high it was with daisies! And a pond in the bottom field. The poppies! Oh, it was glorious!"

Her strange, deaf voice. Disembodied. It could have been blown then from the bottom field, carried up through the years on the wind, pulled out of shape by time and distance but still the words there to tell it: the wheat that rustled huskily about the children's ears, the poppies' silky blood against their knees, the heavy may clouding the hedgerows, sweet cicely like a spray of water up from the wheels in the lane. Voices. They flew like birds from the corn stalks. While the bright clouds bowled.

She made to turn back but Morgan would hear more. "Yes. And we went to the Highcliffe," she said. "Every year." The details spinning now, like baby spiders travelling on the wind, each thread to form the whole again, like candy floss, like those late summer clouds. "Oh it was something then. All along the promenade the smell of seaweed. And down below, the sand so hot it burned our feet. We used to run into the water then. And Punch and Judy. Threepence! The sad donkeys that bit. Who could blame them? Ah, but there was that summer that lasted so long."

"Yes, you told us." Morgan would have preferred to hear more about the sad donkeys. She knew what was coming.

"A summer full of wasps and rotting plums and maggots in the meat. When the children sickened. Oh you can't tell me it was the maggots. Diptheria they tried to tell us it was, but I wouldn't have it. I still won't have it. It was the stench of what was coming, blowing back on us from up ahead, blowing them all away, the children. Like our Bridget. She would have been ninety-one, no, ninety-two this year."

"Yes, you said." But the Old Lady would not be moved until it was finished.

"Ninety-two. I was so proud to have a little sister. But it took her too. Maggots! And she was sent off in her christening gown. A long one, like an angel's hair. I couldn't understand it. They said it was against the law to bury the dead. Cremations only. How could they do that? All the white silk?"

The Old Lady took a great gulp of air and put her hand to her throat as if to work it down. "Or maybe ninety-three," she said. Then she closed her eyes, exhausted by her long speech. Or perhaps by the arithmetic.

"Do you suppose anyone bothered tae tell her about the Day Out?" asked Morgan. "Do her guid tae get out. Look at the state of her."

The Old Lady did indeed look seedy, crumby, as if she might

benefit from a good stiff breeze.

"Ihht's thah Daay Ouut tamah-rhow," said Sherilee, displaying her tonsils again.

Morgan had no patience for this exercise. She led the Old Lady back to her seat and left them to their excruciating exchange while she made desultory efforts to tidy the room and its population of figurines. The Old Lady had an obvious leaning towards shepherds and sweeps; then there were the small boys in lederhosen and the leathery little old men with lasts. And it was true democracy. Received aesthetic worth had no relevance on these shelves where bleary drunks leaned on lamp posts in front of the Tuscany majolica and ch'ing cockerels exalted beside ashtrays from Blackpool.

Morgan moved a pair of Minton candlesticks—Morgan knew about these things—to a more prominent position, and then on a second, more devious thought, moved them back. Her previous experience did not count for nothing.

"Tell her she ought to lock up her valuables while we're gone."

Submissive, laborious, Sherilee did as she was told, word for word.

"She ought tae keep them out of harm's way. Anyone could break in."

"—of haarm's waay. Anyone cuuhld braay—"

It was like trying to speak on one of the old transatlantic telephone lines with a bad echo. Morgan waited for Sherilee to finish.

"I know, I know," the Old Lady said. "You're quite right of course."

"Tell her I could put them in the safe—" The word was a lit fuse. Sparks crackled, "—for her," Morgan finished slowly, thinking.

"Puuht them ihhn—" But the Old Lady was no longer deaf. Before Sherilee had finished she turned and looked Morgan in the eye. And perhaps could hear the fuse hiss, though she need not have feared it. Morgan was no longer thinking of candlesticks.

"You get on with your work," the Old Lady said. "I'll look after my collection. And draw that curtain."

She reached for a plate of sweetbreads, popped one in her mouth and resumed her chewing. Belinda began to salivate like a cat.

"Oh, bloody hell," said Morgan. "I've had enough of this. Will there be anything else, Ma'am?"

The Old Lady shook her head so violently that a piece of meat fell onto her chest.

"No."

Morgan and Sherilee left.

"You're up to something," said Sherilee, smitten with a rare stroke of insight.

"Up for something. Up for anything. If only I could have a goddamn drink."

The Dining Room

Tots had had an idea. "I'll show you where some is."

Turnip wine was not the most enticing bribe Tots could think of but it was all she could come up with at the moment. "Please," she said. "There's six bottles. Please." Morgan, megalithic at the gong, paused. Tots, she could tell, had never purloined anything in her life. Still, never too old to learn, never too late to start.

She was touched; most people tried to stop her drinking. Besides, although there was a Government-subsidised distillery still in operation, her habit was becoming almost too expensive to support. Not that she would have done it for that, not for booze, not even for money. With Morgan it was never the payoff. If Morgan took on a job it was for the cerebral workout and the resulting injections of neat adrenalin that took her higher than any old fermented malt—or turnip—ever could. And this Tots, well ... Morgan had a photograph of herself at the same age; she was at the back door of her grandmother's house. The photograph had been intended for her mother. They didn't let children in at visiting times. She was wearing a dark sweater from which her bony wrists protruded too far, as if somewhere higher up inside the sleeves she might be holding sticks that worked a pair of false hands. Her socks were wrinkled. Someone had cut her black hair in a lopsided fashion—for a wee bit of style. She could remember how her fingers had itched to grab the scissors and do the same for the offending hairdresser.

"All right. You've got me. But I'm a heavy sleeper, mind. You'll have tae wake me yourself. Two o'clock."

"I won't even go to sleep." And even her teeth might have been pleased, the way they displayed themselves.

"Watch yourself, then," said Morgan and Tots ducked and disappeared as the maid took a mighty swing at the gong for dinner.

The reverberations had barely ceased when a glistening brown crocodile toecap hit the top stair at the same moment as the door of Mrs. Pinnacle's apartment clicked open.

The Master waited. "My dear," he said.

Mrs. Pinnacle smiled. She was happy in her work. Together they went down to dinner.

In the dining room, four large jacks holding up the ceiling proposed palatial space with their suggestion of columns.

The pargeting was heavy with grapes and vine leaves. Some of the molding had broken from the wide borders and lay around the edges of the room like chunks of icing from a wedding cake. But it was at least something to marvel at since the windows had been boarded up.

The Master sat at one end of the table, the Mistress at the other; they waited. The children had been given tea. George was not back. Mr. Hawkin was always an hour late and the Old Lady would eat in her room. Mr. and Mrs. Pinnacle preferred it that way.

"Well. I wonder what delights ...."

"Yes indeed."

"The croquettes were good yesterday."

"Exceptional."

"They always are."

"Always."

"As they should be."

"Ah."

Sherilee carried in the watercress soup, said, "Bon appertea," as Mrs. Phelum had taught her to and left.

"It will be fine for tomorrow."

"Yes."

"A fine day."

"Mm."

"For a day out."

"They should be pleased."

"They should be. And grateful."

The Master, his head bent to his soup, his eyes until that moment fixed on the laptop he had positioned in place of a napkin, raised one eyebrow and shot a glance at Mrs. Pinnacle. She still made slips.

Mrs. Pinnacle, genteelly sipping, was not aware. She was at times like this in love with her work. It had its drawbacks (didn't all jobs) and the children were several of them, (the rough knees, the teeth that dangled). But the perks! She had only to look across the table and she would be looking right at one. He was a gold mine. Mention a raise, merely mention it, and he was on the keyboard. She smiled at him but now he had abandoned his soup and was entering new instructions with both hands. She was taken for granted, just like a real wife. But she'd worked for it. She'd made herself useful if not indispensable. And yet, to think she had almost walked away that first day.

Sherilee removed the soup plates and Morgan, in whose head the gong had not yet stopped, brought in the chicken Kiev. The Master jabbed one more key and resumed his meal.

She had had such grave misgivings when she started. Having heard the rumours. Nothing explicit, only hints and innuendo, insinuations here and there. Something about the number of children the wife had borne being unequal to the number she had.

"Good?"

"Very."

"Good."

Something about her appetite. But in the end Virginia Pinnacle, or Virginia Pirstine as she was known then, decided not to go delving into all that. She belonged to the Nanny agency, not to the Ministry of Intelligence or whatever they were called. And besides she could not bear to think about all that side of things. What his wife did with her babies was all the same to Virginia. Nothing could match the fundamental abomination of her having given birth in the first place.

Sherilee came in again for the plates and Morgan, with some ceremony, because it was the result of an expensive and clandestine deal somewhere round Charing Cross, followed with the heart, arranged tastefully on a bed of Haggerty's onions.

"Ah, heart."

"Your favourite."

"My favourite."

How Virginia Pirstine had come in the first place to belong to the Nanny agency had been something of an accident. Nannihood was the last but one card that she would willingly have drawn. Nursing was the last. She could not bear the bleeding noses and leaking wounds of nine-year-olds. She could still remember when, at about their age, she had fallen out of, or more accurately, down, a pear tree, grazing the length of her arm on the bark of the trunk as she reached for a hold. At the bottom she had sat and looked at her arm, which felt as if it had been plunged in snow. It looked hardly different from the other, only whiter. But as she continued to look, the blood began to appear in minute pinpricks that multiplied in the manner of raindrops, closer and closer together until they began to puddle and pool and she had become horribly aware of the autonomous existence of all the wet and sticky parts inside her that would continue willy-nilly to seep and flow, pulsate and quiver ungovernably. Appalled but determined not to be implicated, she had fainted clean away, unaware that four years later she would be required to perform this escape feat monthly, or learn to contemplate the sight of blood. She chose to faint and for the next several years suffered her adolescence like epilepsy. When she was twenty-one her life changed. Fourth and fifth opinions in the medical profession agreed and Virginia Pirstine was scooped out like a melon. Recovering nine months later, she bought a bottle of Bollinger and toasted her new self.

Thus unburdened, Virginia Pirstine felt she could safely embark on a career; she answered a newspaper advertisement for a highly paid administrative assistant. The successful applicant, it stated, would be widely experienced and highly efficient, long on skills, low in tolerance of mediocrity and hot on punctuality. Virginia thought it sounded just like her. Unaware that she had copied down the box number for the adjacent advertisement—*Nannies/Wet-nurses Required*—she sent a reply expounding at length on her aptitude for organization, her facility with communication skills, familiarity with the newest technology and keen interest in the latest in systems organization. The Master snapped her up.

"Right," he had said when she walked in. In her suit. "Capital."

For years he had been struggling with his wife's, Cali's, increasingly earthy and animal ways. What had first attracted him now repelled; her essential difference, her otherness had begun, as soon as she became pregnant, to exclude him and to feed upon itself. His rare flower had metamorphosed into a gangling ravenous, chaotic creature, flinging out tentacles to catch at anyone or anything that might serve its purpose.

Fastening cufflinks he fretted. He could not take her anywhere. She had become an embarrassment, with her dishevelled hair and leaky breasts. "Leave them at home," he would say (referring to the babies). But she would not. Donning a sling where other women flung fur. "They have to eat," she would reply. Calling on truth. "You did."

So urgent and heartfelt was the plea he sent to Nanette's Nannies that an appointment was immediately arranged with the first applicant drawn at random.

"Capital," he had said. And Virginia had glowed, tugging at the jacket.

"But let me take you to my wife. You'll be working with her, after all."

"Ah," said Virginia.

Cali had stared. Her eyelids were heavy with scorn.

"Show me your breasts," she had said, finally.

"Ah," said Virginia again. "Aha."

"I'll leave you two then," said the Master, "to get on with it."

When he returned the matter was resolved.

"She's hired," said Cali. "Mrs. Phelum's showing her to her room."

A deal had obviously been struck. Without him. No matter. For the first time in years the Master warmed to his wife. He had not expected such an easy victory. "I'll take you out," he said. "This very night. My treasure. My ruby." He kissed her ear, trying not to snuff up patchouli. "Eight o'clock."

And at eight o'clock Virginia Pirstine was waiting for him in an emerald green acetate cocktail dress and navy blue high heels. She clutched a slim purse.

Without missing a beat, the Master had offered her his arm, surprised only that he had not thought of this splendid arrangement himself.

By the end of the first week Virginia Pinnacle, as she had taken to calling herself, had deposited a week's salary in her underwear drawer and assumed all wifely duties but one, while Cali had begun again darkly, deliciously to brood, sliding ever deeper into sensual dreams of motherhood.

The Master had straightened his tie and put his foot down. He had tucked away the procreative instrument in the neat boxer shorts and withdrawn his services utterly. The more he thought about it, the more sense it made. His wife had no business bringing children into the world. She was a liability; she was going downhill, like other people's share prices, and getting worse daily. She wore what amounted to fancy dress and lived without furniture, lolling about, sleeping, even eating on the floor. And they all ate with their fingers—when they did eat; most of them had their heads inside her dress until they were five. He had not realized how bad it was getting until he heard one of the nursing so-called infants in the kitchen asking for corned beef and pickled onions. She let the children do just as they pleased. They ate and slept and slept and excreted not when it was appropriate but whenever it suited them. She was unfit. It was just fortunate that she had given up going out. In fact, if she hadn't, he was not sure he wouldn't have forbidden it. And so, just to be sure, he did. "Who needs it?" said his wife, not without ambiguity—and knowing that he certainly did. Before too long he had invested in a host of accessories with which to enliven certain dreary encounters—stringy hair and a whiff of sour dish cloth being no longer enough to titillate. His wife on the other hand appeared to need nothing and no one—apart from the babies—least of all him. Incredulous, he had watched as his wife grew obscenely, horrifically pear-shaped again, basking in her courtyard with her back against the warm brick, ripening her belly in the sun.

Then he was doubly glad to have found a respectable substitute; not that he believed anything would come of it, this immaculate conception. Even when he heard her crooning and lowing in labour that morning, he had not believed, thinking—hoping—the thing would die before it could draw a breath.

He sat and watched resolutely as the labour progressed. Cali made a point of managing each birth herself, asking only that Mrs. Phelum be there to attend her. He on the other hand made a point of avoiding each occasion. But not this one. As the hour approached, however, he found himself overcome by a sensation stronger than his resolution; it might have been fear, he did not recognise it, but he was grateful for the old copy of the *Times* that lay near the cat box. He snatched it up and held it open to his face, wishing he could vanish behind it. "Mr. Pinnacle! Quick or you'll miss it!" Mrs. Phelum had all but to wrench it from his hands. And when the moment came he had to look. A dark head crowned with blood. It eased, it eased, and it burst into the world, its eyes squeezed shut. He had watched transfixed as it blinked once and seemed to concentrate, then all was motion. A shoulder, an arm—it seemed to wave at him—and out it came whole, thrashing.

"Haaa-ha!" it shouted. And it sounded like laughter.

It was a girl.

His wife shuddered violently and bared her teeth. She leaned forward, her hair raining darkness on the child, mercifully hiding what she did to the cord with her teeth, and scooped it out of the puddle it lay in and up onto the smooth slopes of her breast, lying back again in a naked orgasm of ecstasy. She had done it!

He drew nearer, intending to whisper some curse in her ear. He was enraged. And she, opening one eye, saw it. In a spasm of malice she pulled the infant from the nipple on which it had latched and pushed it into his pin-striped arms, blood, caul, and all.

"For you, darling," she said, and lay back delighted with herself.

"Whatever next!" Mrs. Phelum with a warm blanket bustled. "You'll kill her with kindness, you two. Give her to me." And she took the child, folding it expertly in the blanket.

"For you," repeated Cali, grinning.

"She's none of mine." His mouth had become beaky with gall.

"My gift—"

"Your monster."

"To you."

"You keep it."

Mrs. Phelum pretended not to hear. She tucked in the last corner of wrap. "There you go, tots," she said. "Now which one of you wants her?"

Cali rolled over and sat up, pulling a quilt round her shoulders. "We have to clean up," she said. "Take her away."

The Master and Virginia Pinnacle finished their heart at the same moment. Their forks chimed.

"Very nice."

"Wasn't it."

The napkins at their mouths, blotting traces.

How many knew or now remembered the whole story it is difficult to say. Virginia Pinnacle had heard of course. No matter what they said afterwards about doorsteps and abandoned babies, she had still heard, literally. She had lain in the room next door to the Mistress's with her head under a pillow. In the interests of decorum she had tried not to listen. Then she had tried to listen. What had begun by coasting with low throaty moans in and out of faint desire had gone barrelling down stretches of desperate urgency. Virginia was appalled. If they should need another pair of hands .... She got up and locked the door and then she went back and put her head under the pillow again. But still she had heard. And the hair on her scalp had lifted when the voice finally soared and left the rails, flying high in blue silence, the baby shouting down below. Found on the doorstep!

And then there was Mrs. Phelum who did most certainly know and, though she was not very good with dates, remembered—remembered in fact a great deal more than the Master would have wished. For Mrs. Phelum could recall how, when she returned to her kitchen half an hour later, she found the Master waiting for her. He had changed his suit and was standing by the great pine table, in the middle of which lay the newborn, balanced on its side in the expert swaddling like a sausage roll.

"I can't be seen with this," he said.

"What are you talking about?" Mrs. Phelum was indignant on behalf of the child.

"I can't be seen with this," he repeated. "You'll know what to do." He took out a wad of bank notes about the thickness of a cheese sandwich and placed it beside the child, "I expect."

Mrs. Phelum's chest expanded and her lips drew invisible purse strings tight. "Oh, no," she said. "No chance."

The Master ignored her and bent to pick up a large black briefcase. He opened it and went to put the baby in. "I'll leave the ... other," with the smallest movement of his face in the direction of the cheese sandwich, "for you. Only remember: there is no child."

"Oh, yes there is, and you better not touch it." Moral ardour was not one of Mrs. Phelum's prevailing passions but now she burned with it. "Don't matter how many wads of that stuff you put on the bleedin' table, you won't get me playing your little game. And you better watch your step or I'll broadcast—yes, that's what I'll do— I'll *broadcast* everything I heard up them stairs. Everything. The lot. Now I don't care if this is one of yours or not, but you can't tell me it's not one of hers. So just you think again. Least you can do is give it a roof." It did not seem quite enough. "And a home. And a hearth."

The Master sat down. The hated baby might be disposed of but there was no briefcase in the world big or black enough to dispose of Mrs. Phelum. "A man in my position," he began, "whose wife—"

"You don't have to *advertise* it. I won't tell. You can adopt it, make it legal. Say you found it on the doorstep."

The Master raised his eyebrows a fraction.

"One more won't make no difference. More the merrier. Another mouth to feed. You already got the nanny."

But Mrs. Phelum had gone too far. The Master had his calculator in the palm of his hand and was tickling the truth out of it. To pay someone to look after the outcome of his wayward wife's infernal hanky-panky! To feed it! Out of his own pocket!

"Well you can always put her to work when she's old enough. Then she pays for herself."

Again the levitating eyebrows. Here was an idea.

"Or before. Thank you Mrs. Phelum. Where did you say you found this baby?"

"On the doorstep, sir. This morning."

"Right. Well I'll make the appropriate arrangements. Keep an eye on it till then will you, Mrs. Phelum?" Already he could see the bond he would draw up and was filling it with constraints and conditions.

"All right. But only this one. No more. You can't expect me to produce eight course meals with the place full of babies."

"No indeed. Goodbye now, Mrs. Phelum."

Mrs. Phelum eyed the baby on the table and decided on jam roly-poly for pudding.

"Thank you, no," said Virginia Pinnacle to Sherilee, who yawned as she offered treacle tart. "Or perhaps just a little."

Their forks gummed in amber crumbs, sticky. It was not advisable to say more than 'mm'.

"Mm."

"Mm."

They were a double act Pirstine and Pinnacle. Always in step, attuned.

The hapless Tots in the confusion of the kitchen had been all but forgotten. She had lain around on the kitchen table amid the sausages and dumplings for several weeks. Virginia Pinnacle would have nothing to do with her. She said she had made her arrangements with the Mistress. She said she wasn't going to do two jobs and the Master would have to speak to the Mistress about it. But the Master had already spoken to the Mistress and taken his revenge like a long cool draught, saying he had 'seen to' the baby and would 'see to' any others if she cared to make an issue of it.

So Mildred, who had just started and seemed to show a special aptitude for tasks requiring little exertion, was called upon to hold a bottle of formula to the desperate mouth.

Upstairs, the great carved doors remained shut. Cali languished. She was bereft. Her husband had murdered her very soul. She was adrift on a sea of loneliness, awash with loss—until she found she was pregnant again.

It was on the very morning that news of the Mishap shook the world awake, that this new thought came to Cali.

"Have you heard?" her husband asked, ashen, thinking of all the dead consumers, the markets like deserts.

"I don't need to," she answered, thinking of urinalaysis, "I know. I'm pregnant again."

Then once more for Cali nothing else mattered. Tots was forgotten along with all the rest. She did not exist. To be in the company of her children or not, Cali did not care. All that mattered was the lusciously, the miraculously swelling moonbelly. While the rest of the world slowly fell to pieces in the aftermath, she cared for her belly with utter devotion, exquisite tenderness, annointing it with oil morning and night, massaging it hourly and hourly meditating upon its wonder. Filled full again she was fulfilled. For four years, through all the Solid Winter, she remained in this state of nirvanic bliss, though whether it was the same pregnancy or one of a series no one knew. Meanwhile the rest of the household shakily picked up the pieces of what they had always fondly called normal life and resumed a rough approximation of it.

A deception well-executed soon becomes an institution. It will not be gainsaid. Even the perpetrators believe; or perhaps especially. Virginia Pinnacle was the greatest believer of all. For her there was no distinction now between her life and her work. She lived her work. Not that it was a conscious decision, to deceive, only an expedience. At that early stage in her career it became increasingly easy to let misunderstandings stand. "Ah, Mrs. Pinnacle! I've so much looked forward to meeting you ...." "Ralph has told me all about you, Mrs. Pinnacle ...." "Mrs. Pinnacle?" The right thing to say was, more than ever, a comfort in these cold times, with the pigeons dead upon the ground like leaves, the furniture burning in the grate. And so Virginia Pinnacle learned to smile, nod, sympathize, protest and even raise an eyebrow all on cue. And never a hair out of place. Where some had none. It was amazing how she did it. After how many? And kept her figure too. Marvellous really. Time and again the Master congratulated himself on his selection, and time and again Virginia Pinnacle as she tucked away her pay, thanked her lucky star that had provided her with a place when she had not thought to seek one.

To begin with she had worried that the children, the drawbacks, as she thought of them, might be a problem. But the Master followed the long-established custom of removing children early to educational establishments where they would be taught to forget. On the rare occasions that any of them returned, it was evident that the educational process was successful. A sad bewilderment on the faces of the younger ones showed that they had already learned not to ask questions; the older ones would simply smile and say she looked wonderful, showing their commendable progress towards the goal of paramnesia. Virginia Pinnacle felt reasonably secure. Though it was not foolproof. There were holidays and other exigencies, times, as now, with Ben and Gordon at home, when there would be no choice but to plump the lumpy pillow or pat the lonely shoulder. And she would wonder how she had come to be there among the snot-streaked pyjamas and what had become of the executive suite in chrome and corduroy and plenty of speckled grey that she had envisaged when she applied for the job. How she would hanker then for the male odour of dry-cleaning and shoe leather and ash!

But still it was tolerable and a small price to pay for an assured place and the role of leading lady. What was not tolerable and what Virginia dreaded more than her designated duties were the unregulated encounters, the chance meetings with the children. For while at the appointed times they were content to call her mother, they seemed, surprised on stairs or in doorways, to look her in the eye and say, "I know. I know and you know." She could see it there. They looked right into her and said, "Imposter. Impossible mother. Not mother. Though we pretend to have forgotten we have not. The taste of her milk is in our mouths." It was unnerving.

And now there was Tots. Who was asking questions. Found on the doorstep; Virginia Pinnacle thirteen years ago was too new to say differently. But they were all in it together, it seemed. At the time she had thought fleetingly of speaking up. But, afterwards, everything changed; a place was a place; she was not stupid. Mr. Pinnacle probably had his reasons. Though she wished his solution were less visible. As Tots grew, scrappy and spindly and runny-nosed, so Virginia Pinnacle's discomfort grew. It was like having one's conscience walking around on two legs. But she learned to ignore it.

"Shall I bring the cheese, sir?" There never was cheese but it was a comforting ritual.

"Not tonight, thank you." He turned to Virginia. "If that's all right with you?"

"Quite all right."

But very satisfying that the girl had remembered to ask. There were appearances. And a wife in navy wool. It mattered.

"That will be all."

"Coffee for me. If you don't mind."

The Master looked up sharply. Sometimes, he thought, Virginia Pinnacle took advantage of her position, went too far. But that was always the way: when it came to people, there were always drawbacks.

"Very good, Madam." Sherilee, who would have preferred to say 'Okey-doke,' had at least learned her lines.

The Plumbing

T ots woke herself up at two the next morning. She had no clock but she did have a perfect sense of duration and judged the passage of hours and minutes with atomic accuracy, even in her sleep. For her personal alarm to function she had only to repeat the desired time of waking as she lay down. Then her sleep was of an entirely special character. No unexpected free-falls from high buildings. It was dreamless. It could almost be said not to exist at all. There was no dark swamp filled with doppelgangers and lumpy pillows. She could make the leap from one moment to another, predetermined moment away in the distant morning in a single bound. Nodding and waking were the twin blades of shears; they lopped off the intervening stretch of time. At two o'clock, then, on the dot, Tots snapped awake, eyes flying open, limbs flexed.

She put on her sweater over her yellowed nightdress and slipped barefoot out of her room.

The House was far from quiet. It seemed as if after a heavy day holding things up it might have lost interest. An uneasy creaking issued steadily from its joists and was punctuated by sudden small catastrophes as things slid and fell or pinged and gave way, but these were always unremarked at the time and rarely discovered later, minor events in the elsewhere.

The pipework on the other hand was engaged as always in its endless struggle with the forces of nature. A distant knocking could be heard coming from some further reach of the House, but even as Tots listened, the noise grew louder and the knocking quickened to a thundering rattle bearing down on her like an invisible steam engine about to burst through the walls. She ducked.

In fact the plumbing in itself was a force to be reckoned with and interaction with any of its parts was never undertaken without a degree of circumspection. The handles of taps for instance might turn with no warning at all into dangerous projectiles and the cistern in the downstairs cloakroom had a habit of silently filling whenever the water level in the bowl was raised, so that the unwary, settling in for ten minutes peace and quiet, might find their feet in a rising tide of rusty water. The Master of course had his own fixtures installed in his magnificent ensuite boasting an antique water closet in hand-painted french porcelain with a gilt-edged seat. But it could not save him from the perversities of the system. Not many weeks had passed after its installation before two rats and a toad found their way up the pipe to splash uncertainly in the painted bowl. The Master had the lid nailed down. Where he relieved himself was as much a mystery as the matter of his net worth.

Tots stood and listened to the knocking pipe come to rest, making sure that its noise had not disguised any other movement. The plumbing she realized had deteriorated since Mr. Creighton-Wallace had stopped coming. At this very moment she could hear the constant, ineludible plink of unstopped water right above her head. But it really didn't matter; there was a constant slow dripping wherever one stood. It came not only from the taps, which were uniformly leaky, but from every bend and joint in the pipes themselves. And it was getting worse. The escaped water trickled in hidden places, working wood to cheesy softness and running away to cut under the foundations. Only Roger the cat had ever taken an interest in the plumbing. Roger had spent many happy hours in the darkness under floors and behind walls. He knew the places where he could wander in around the pipes, stopping to lick at a drip here, a drop there and warming his toes as he went. It may well be that he found the lead solution preferable to the lethal cocktail that passed for rainwater outside. Or perhaps he had thought himself in a subterranean rainforest licking the warm raindrops from the sinuous limbs of ancient trees. No one had noticed his spitting when he trod on a pipe hotter than the rest. The plumbing spat all the time. And sputtered and whistled and banged. It would not be much longer before a replacement for Mr. Creighton-Wallace would have to be found.

Before the Mishap, Norman Creighton-Wallace had made a handsome living in gynaecology, mining female cavities for riches. They had been happy days for him; not that he loved the female body, indeed he had in his early days felt himself constrained by his distaste to wear dark glasses while in consultation and later, as his aversion grew, to hire an assistant to kneel between the stirrups and peer inside, reporting sightings or guiding the movements of his instruments. No, it was not that he had any affection for the cases upon which he worked, it was just that they were so ... fruitful. They were his easy lays, submitting to his rubber gloves that snipped and snapped, scooped and grafted, filled and drywalled at two hundred and thirty seven pounds an hour. Halcyon days. But the Mishap changed everything; whole shoals of clients were left stranded on the mud flats of a new poverty; there simply were not enough rich people to service. And, strangely, after it happened, especially in the days of the big Scare, those who could have children thought themselves lucky—and so did those who couldn't.

Seeing his appointment book lying yellowed on his secretary's desk, Mr. Creighton-Wallace had been obliged to close his office, sell his pigskin chair and lock up his instruments in the bathroom cabinet until such time as business should pick up again. The loss of his practice might not in itself have brought him grief, but the collapse of the stock market was a death blow. Mr. Creighton-Wallace was forced to look for work.

It was hard to say whether he was good plumber. He enjoyed

tinkering for the sound it made, was moved by the throb and rush of water through the pipes and celebrated small successes by opening (as he had been wont to do after a difficult hysterectomy) one of his better wines. He was certainly happy and always pleased to call. Which was just the point: he was almost always there—a fact which could only cast doubt on his aptitude and lead one to wonder whether he might not have overlooked some small consideration, a valve or a drain-cock, the time before. "If he's so red hot an' all that ..." Mrs. Phelum tucked her chins into her chest for this, "...if he's so red hot, how come he has to keep coming back?" She raised an eyebrow. She didn't have to spell it out, did she? And yet it was the day she spoke those very words that Mr. Creighton-Wallace found a motive for coming more often and Mrs. Phelum a reason to let him.

He was that day investigating a short pipe which with its own shut-off valve protruded inexplicably from the floor of the middle landing. After making several minor adjustments to taps and valves in the cellar, Mr. Creighton-Wallace returned to the landing, turned the handle of the valve and cocked his head to listen for sounds of approaching success. The ensuing geyser of rusty boiling water that hit him in the ear rendered him partially deaf for the rest of his life.

More immediately it brought, or his howls brought, Mrs. Phelum hurrying up from the kitchen. Greatly affected by the sight of Mr. Creighton-Wallace spattered with what seemed to be blood, Mrs. Phelum, who had been preparing one of the black market flounder that had been washing up at Southend, felt compelled to clasp the plumber to her and press the chilly fish to his wounded ear. Still holding his head, she backed onto a chair and sat down bringing him to his knees beside her. Cradled in this manner on Mrs. Phelum's swelling ocean of breast and suffering still from shock, Mr. Creighton-Wallace was quickly rendered delirious. In her compassion Mrs. Phelum rocked, shifting the silt of Norman's memory back and forth in ever deepening arcs uncovering layer beneath layer until at last he glimpsed visions from an earlier time, when laps were for sitting on and breasts were consolation.

The motion, the scent of flour and fish, the soft huffing sympathy from Mrs. Phelum's nostrils—Norman was inflamed. Or perhaps it was the tautness of the white apron over her spread knees that so strongly evoked his former profession. In any case Norman's right hand with robotic speed and precision shot up between her welcoming thighs and settled in the warm smile waiting there, as if it were the only place he had been searching for in all his long years of practice. "Whatever it takes, darlin'," said Mrs. Phelum. "Whatever it takes." She was beginning to feel faint.

Mrs. Phelum, whose body had often enough dispensed its solace to those in need, but whose spirit had never for a moment been unfaithful to her husband, or even her husband's memory, now found herself beginning to participate. Norman was so ... at home. Mrs. Phelum was helpless. With difficulty she disengaged him and drove him to the pantry where they made an extraordinary kind of love next to a case of Meow Mix.

After that Mrs. Phelum became noticeably coy with other men and boys, while Norman began wilfully to sabotage the hot water system in order to ensure a steady stream of opportunities. It was Mrs. Phelum's rightful and long overdue affair of the heart. But it did not last.

There came the day, one hot day in summer, when, with his good ear pressed to the clammy surface of a cold water pipe, Norman inadvertently overheard a sizzling hot tip. The Master was discussing the new electricity allowances for food depots and the need for air-conditioning. Norman Creighton-Wallace borrowed two hundred pounds from Mrs. Phelum, painted ELECTRICIAN over the word PLUMBER on his van and was off.

Mrs. Phelum said, "Easy come, easy go," and got on with the jam.

Morgan's Room

T ots knocked at the door for the third time. She could still hear snoring on the other side. She turned the handle quietly and peered round the door. Moonlight leaked through the torn curtain. Sherilee lay in the bed on the far side with the covers up to her chin. Most of the time when she was awake she wore a look of steady concentration, as if she were learning a part. Now she looked purposefully content; she knew how to sleep.

Morgan's covers were on the floor. She lay face down, languid in the glamour of black silk, one arm over the edge of the bed. She was snoring loudly.

"Wake up!" Tots shook her arm and Morgan rolled over, frowning.

"Oh, Christ!" She rubbed her nose viciously. "You remembered."

"Course I did. Come on."

Sherilee made a small bubbling sound and drew the covers still higher.

"Come on."

Morgan sat up, sighing, the black silk sliding under caffè latte satin as she put on a gown. She reached under the bed and pulled out a pair of heavy, steel-toed boots, which she proceeded to put on.

"You can get anything you want wi' a pair of these on your feet." She dragged a battered Gucci grip out from under the bed and stood up.

"Right," she said. "Let's crack the bugger open." At the top of the cellar steps they lit candles to preserve the precious batteries in Morgan's flashlight. In the dark, the vapours of putrefaction and mold that by day had merely lurked congregated openly. Tots was glad she was not alone.

They stopped in front of the red front door.

"You didn't know I was a member of the exclusive Platinum Five Hundred K Club, did you?"

Tots was ready to be impressed. Morgan flashed the card. "It means dick."

But the card all the same slipped in beside the strike plate, there was a click, and the door opened.

The parlour maid put her bag on top of the safe.

"O.K., now. This shouldn't be too difficult. Just a wee old Brigstock. Built like a bank but blows out like a wet fart."

"Blows?"

"Well. We'll have tae see. That might be a wee bit excessive; we'll start off easy and just see how we go. Here, hold this." Morgan handed Tots a thin wire and took out a small hand drill. "Only diamond I own," she said as she fitted the bit and began to drill.

From time to time she spat on the bit and it sizzled. For the rest of the time she whistled *The Bonnie Light Horseman* through her teeth. Over and over. And over. Tots began to think she might not take to a life of crime after all.

"Now. When I say 'now' you just take a hold of that wee end and stick it in that wee hole there, O.K.? Hold on, I'll just get this turned—there—now! Is it in?"

"Sort of."

"No, no, no. Put it in all the way."

Tots squeezed her eyes shut to concentrate. Something slipped aside and the wire went in.

"Good. Now hold tight tae this dial while we do the next one. Got it? Don't let it move or you'll snap off the wire."

Morgan drilled again and they repeated the procedure. At the end of an hour the main lock bristled with wires.

"Ready?" said Morgan.

Tots was ready for bed. "What for?"

"The boots, dear." Morgan stood up and stepped back. "Mind out." She aimed a kick at the side of the safe and the door flew open on twenty years of unpaid bills and final demands. There was no mistaking them, crisp in their smooth manila sliding over one another, handled hardly at all, most of them unopened. Morgan reached in further. There were only wads of old fivers that the Master had not been quick enough to spend.

"Is it them?" Tots asked, knowing that it was not.

"Oh, shit," said Morgan. She had shovelled the piles of envelopes out onto the floor and there it was, an inner compartment, sealed tight. "It's one o' *them.*"

She sat back on her haunches and looked at Tots. "It ca'nae be done. Not wi'out a bang. It'll have tae wait."

"That's a blow," said Tots, jocose while her tear ducts burned. She laughed feebly.

Morgan was caught off guard. She had expected reproach. "Let's put this rubbish back and get tae bed," she said. Even before she got back to her room, Morgan knew she would not be able to sleep. Old memories were stirred; they bobbed on the surface like cherries in gin. She could feel the waxy wrapping round the wad of heavy, soft plastic, smell the copper wire and the fine oil on the sliding plate. It was as provocative as the smell of musk.

She went in quietly and got down on the floor by her bed, pulling herself under like a garage mechanic. The package was there where she had tied it under the springs, her own passport to freedom when she wanted it. She untied it and wriggled out. Sherilee turned over on her side and curled herself into a ball.

Going downstairs, conscious now of the heavy boots, Morgan reflected that she had not had a drink for about thirteen hours. Adrenalin was a good substitute for alcohol. On a job her brain took corners on two wheels, slicing all the edges and cutting up the back streets, while her body, still in overdrive, hummed.

And there was the weight in her pocket. Oh, so much of it and she needed so little. She was almost delirious with the possibility of excess.

In the cellar, she took a sheet of black plastic from her bag and spread it on the ground beside the safe. She laid out the parts in order of assembly and unwrapped the paper package, placing the contents in the centre covered lightly with the brown wrapping, like ham sandwiches at a picnic. Then she set to work on the inner compartment.

She really did need such a very little, a morsel, a sliver, about the same amount, were it cheese, that you would set in a mouse-trap.

Which left all the rest. Which she thought about. She wondered if she had the appetite. The plans, the careful preparation, the precarious manipulation of time and space, deadly dodges. Each job an expedition. It was like climbing, step by tentative step, the side of a giant fuel tank, only to stand on the rim and lob one in. Then the mad slithering scramble to safety—or maybe not—before the blow.

"Morgan, isn't it?"

Still crouching, but turning her head slightly, Morgan could just make out over her right shoulder, the brown calf-skin slippers, the marbled ankles and hairless shins, the maroon silk dressing gown. She did not look any further.

"It is, sir."

"No need to ask what you're doing. The only question now is what to do about it."

"You apprehend me, don't you?" Morgan stood up and tightened the sash at her waist. "A citizen's arrest, isn't it?"

"Perhaps." The Master went over to the safe. He let the toe of his slipper nuzzle the bits and pieces spread on the plastic sheet. "What were you going to use to set it off."

"Just a timer. Set for thirty seconds," she added. The pleasure of seeing his mouth gape. "I mean, I was going tae set it for thirty seconds. I haven't finished yet."

His jaw sprang back and he snapped it shut to hide the terror he had exposed. He peered into the safe, hiding his face while his pulse rate returned to normal. "You could of course set it for whatever time you wished?"

"On a twenty-four hour timer, yes." The old bugger, thought

Morgan.

He picked up the sliver of explosive she had cut.

"How much damage will that do?" His train of thought evident, dribbling now from the corners of his mouth.

"Just enough."

"And that?" he lifted the wrapper on the rest.

"A whole bloody lot."

His mouth twitched and he snuffed up a breath of the fetid air as if he had just arrived at the coast. He paced about behind Morgan for a while without saying anything, watching her back the whole time. Then at last he came round to face her.

"Now you listen to me carefully, Miss Morgan, because I'm not going to repeat any of this. There will be no discussion. You will follow my instructions after listening to everything I have to say. If you carry them out, I shall be quite prepared to overlook this little...'lapse' of yours." The man thought he was in a James Bond movie for God's sake. "If not...."

"Och, let's not bother wi' 'if not.' I hate consequences, don't you? Why don't you just tell me what you want." Though it was obvious.

What the Master wanted, it seemed, above everything else, was a feel of her body. To begin with. But, when he had got that out of his system with a good deal of slippery action inside her wrap (which Morgan, impatient, hastened to a conclusion by lifting her nightgown up to her ears) and after rubbing himself down with a few wads of greasy bank notes, he did finally tell her—and Morgan of course agreed.

A Deviation

S till thinking about Morgan, the Master stopped first at Cali's
apartments on his way back.

"It's me," he said.

"Mmm?"

She was barely awake.

"I'm coming in." As if it were a stronghold to be breached. As it
was.

"Mm."

Damn her. She could not even be bothered to open her eyes.

"I'm coming in to see you in a few minutes. I'll be right back."

Cali slept on. She was woken three minutes later by the intrusion of bony knees between her legs.

"Nngh." He was prising.

She smiled in what he thought was a particularly lewd way. "Hallo, dear," she said. "You're up early."

He did not answer. He was busy rooting around, as if, she thought, he had lost something.

"It's where it always is. Same place all the others keep it."

His look was poison. "Bitch!" he said. But continued to root.

"Have we talked about this?"

"We don't have to. We're married."

"Ah, then you mean this is duty; you're not doing it for pleasure after all."

He thought of suffocating her and changing that.

"I'm giving you a child," he said.

"Ah! You don't have to," she said and braced herself while his anger disembogued. "But thank you for the thought."

"Listen," he said, though he could say nothing more for a moment or two, being out of breath. She was patient. "It's not a thought. You stop feeding that baby as of now, this moment. And you lie still. Don't move a muscle. Even a nursing mother can get pregnant if she lies still afterwards. Thirty-six hours. With you it can't fail."

"Perhaps you could come by to top up?"

"Of—" He caught himself just in time. "Bitch," he said again. Two hours later when she woke and remembered what had happened Cali hooted with laughter and woke the baby.

"So, my pet, my delicious. He wants us to stay home, does he? I wonder why?"

The Bus

J acky the Lackey in boxer shorts and a lime green tank top was up at the crack of dawn. He drove the Mercedes round and parked it in front of the house. Tots was already sweeping the front steps.

"You drivin'?" she asked as he got out and slammed the door.

"You bet. They lookin' fo' class, sister." Clown as well as poet.

"Well you go with the car I suppose," said Tots. And it was true; it was the reason the Mistress had selected him for the job: she liked the look of his black skin under the black hat. In the black car. Only how much nicer if she could get him to wear the rest of the uniform.

"Yeah, they're real colour-conscious, ain't they? Long as they don't get a powder blue limo I'll be O.K., eh? Or white. But, no, you know what really pisses me off? I got to wash it. Wa-shiit!" He opened the door again and sat behind the wheel flexing his fingers and his shoulders.

"What's wrong with that? It's part of the job, innit?"

"You kiddin'?"

"They always do. Chauffers." Her pronunciation stripped the glamour from the job.

"Not this one." And a child appeared from round the corner.

"Round the side, love," said Jacky and in a few moments the child returned with a rag and a pail full of water. Jacky tossed the child a package from the back seat of the car and walked off back to his bed.

The child sat down on the curb and quickly devoured the food in the package.

"You from under the bridge?" asked Tots. In her bleakest moments she thought a cardboard box might be an acceptable alternative to her bedroom in the House, but as soon as there was a clearance she became grateful for her place again. It was an unhealthy prevarication and conducive only to guilt. But she would soon be rid of all that. Her interest today was more than academic.

The child finished swallowing. "They hosed us out. Bastards." She used the word without rancour; it was a convention, a formality like 'Your Honour' or 'Thank you.'

"Bastards," Tots agreed. She had seen them do it once. They used a fire-hose and a bulldozer.

"Bet you had a nice box there, didn't you?" Though she did not mean to patronize.

"I can get another one. Not like the woman what lost her kid."

"Oh, don't tell me," said Tots. And meant it. There were lots of stories. They all ended the same way. But the child would tell this one. She would not be stopped.

"They done it in the morning. When they thought everyone was up, see."

Now Tots's curiosity squirmed under the caterpillar tracks. "Bleeders," she said, but would rather not hear, tried hard not to hear. "Listen I got to go."

"They thought all the dosses was empty. Everyone standin' around. She had only gone for a crap, the mum."

It was not just the baby, it was everyone, herself too, despite her bedroom and her place. The baby was them all. It was why the baby broke her heart.

"I really got to." She would find her courage again, she would. But for now it was safer inside. "Ta-ra."

The girl squatted to take a drink from the bucket and then set to work.

By eight o'clock MacMillan had pulled up in front in his rusty bus, a retired airport shuttle, and the child had secured another job. Her new employer leaned. He found a lamppost and he leaned. It was his favourite pose.

MacMillan, hired by the Master for the day, was still known as the undertaker's man, though he had left that establishment years before the Mishap. Speculation on the reasons for his dismissal had never ceased since that night when Mr. Carter had been observed battering at his own shop door and shouting, "Let me in! There are people who need me in there!" In due course the door had been opened and Mr. Carter had been admitted, only to emerge moments later, white-faced and speechless. Whatever it was he had witnessed between MacMillan and the people who needed him never came to light, but the shock it induced was so great that the speechless condition never passed and Mr. Carter remained mute for the rest of his days. For a short while after the incident, business, as might be expected, suffered a temporary setback, but not for long. Mr. Carter's new condition was found in a perverse manner to enhance the dismal proceedings as he resorted to sign language to ask the most delicate questions and make the most intimate proposals. While Mr. Carter asked them about their requirements, relatives of the deceased rediscovered the potent ritual of mime and found it pleasantly narcotic; word got round. He phrased his questions so beautifully—drawing up a smile with the fingertips of both hands upon his own face, raising his eyebrows, lifting his hair, applying invisible rouge, tilting his head to shave imaginary moustaches. All with the whimsical, quizzical expression of Pierrot. The bereaved were charmed. They found themselves answering in the same manner and went home to write him into their own wills. He had such lovely hands. All in all the experience was wonderfully enriching, except for MacMillan, who was handed his notice in writing. He took the black Mercedes with him. To Mr. Carter it seemed a small price to pay.

But MacMillan wasn't out of work for long. The Mishap saw to that. There was plenty of moonlighting to be had in the aftermath and when things slowed down there was always the odd driving job for those with access to black market fuel. The Master would have liked to have MacMillan for his personal chauffeur but MacMillan would not stoop to service. He spent his days leaning against the gleaming black bodywork, waiting, one ankle crossing the other, one eyebrow raised in perpetual contempt.

That he had handed over the black Merc to Jacky for the day was a mark of the rock solid security of MacMillan's stance of superiority; that he was this morning leaning against the rusted body of an antique airport bus made no difference to him. An automobile, any automotive machine, was simply a vehicle for the expression of his powerful disdain. On the road, where he practised studied ignorance of external objects, moving or not, his sense of superiority could go unchallenged; the sudden appearance of stray cats, the corners of buildings—they were equally insignificant. He drove like a blind man pursued by devils and only in the split second that preceded the point of impact would he deign to recognize an obstacle to his progress. So, cursing, gesturing, taking the most extreme evasive measures, or not taking them, MacMillan when he was not leaning would career through the streets, narrowly missing the halt and the infirm, pursuing the fit and yelling obscenities through the windscreen.

His impatience today to get started did not show. He leaned and waited and trained his supercilious eye on the front door. It opened to reveal an easy target. The day trippers were almost ready and had begun to twitter round the bags and hampers standing in the front hall. The chirruping dwindled to silence as one by one they became conscious of MacMillan's icy stare homing in from the lamp-post. And indeed it might have been mid-winter and they birds freezing to the very branches. No loitering now on the top step, scanning skies for signs of change, a welcome cloud or two, no chummy banter, only a hurried, cowed, bowed descent and a crab-wise approach to the bus, as if anticipating actual bodily harm.

In the safety of the Mercedes Virginia Pinnacle shook her head with a quick, fierce movement as if to rid herself of a bad memory. She smoothed out her gloves on her lap and relaxed. When the Master ducked in beside her she was in heaven. She considered a wifely hand on his knee this birthday morning. But he did not settle back in his seat. He merely lodged one cheek on the edge long enough to say that he had to make a call. Perhaps another morning.

In the bus there was much shuffling and rearranging and a certain amount of deferential coughing. It was customary that in honour of the occasion the family should be represented on the bus. The Master and Mistress relegated to this duty all those with whom they had no wish to travel, a comprehensive list, at the top of which were the children. Uncle George might have been acceptable in the car, they felt—he had a military background—but he could not be persuaded to miss a thigh-thrumming bus ride.

MacMillan shouldered himself from the lamppost and sauntered round to the door of the bus. Jamming his cap lower so that he had to tilt his head to see, he looked at his passengers the way a riot policeman might survey the night's haul.

The cell phone at his belt warbled and the Master's voice crackled through.

"Something has come up, MacMillan. I shall be out of town until further notice. I shall not be joining the party."

"Whatever."

"You go on. Mrs. Pinnacle's driver will be right behind."

"Stuck up old fart," said Scoria. "I knew he wouldn't never come."

"And, Scoria—you are dismissed."

The scullery maid contracted the muscles on one side of her nose and upper lip and her mouth dropped open. She did not say a word but, as if caught when the wind changed, wore the look of sneering perplexity for the first twenty miles. She had thought her place secure, thanks to the Master's indiscretions, now it dawned; all that hanky-panky counted for nothing. It would simply be her word against his and her word, she realized too late, counted for, as she put it, dick.

"Well, well, well," said Morgan. She had not expected him to put in an appearance at all today and surmised that the 'something' had probably come up halfway across the world, at least. Well, what could you expect? A man without scruples. A sudden thought occurred to her.

"Have we got everyone?" she said, standing up.

MacMillan switched on the engine.

"Where's that wet-nurse woman?" said Morgan.

"She's behind us. In the car," said Sherilee. "I saw her come down the front steps just now. After His Lordship got out and went back round the side."

MacMillan hit sixty from a standing start and Morgan had no choice but to sit down. She tried to see the car behind but there was only the smoke from the tires.

"You better be right," she said. She opened her black bag and filled a silver flask from a brand new bottle of Scotch. "I didnae have time this morning," she said. "I was busy. Want some?"

"Not yet." Which could only mean Sherilee was going to have some later. Morgan wondered why she didn't bring her own. Remain philosophical, that was the thing. "Cards!" she said, taking out a pack. "Poker?"

"All right." Sherilee's fear of Morgan's scorn was more powerful than her loathing of card games.

"You don't have to. Not if you've more important things tae attend to."

"Oh, no. I'd like to. I would."

Though what she would have really liked would have been to sit gazing glassy-eyed out of the bus, and picturing shop windows without boards, diamonds and wedding gowns behind the glass, bridesmaid's dresses in lemon with a V at the back and a bow.

"You deal."

"How many?"

Morgan raised her eyes to the dented roof and took out her flask again. "Five, dear, five."

Sherilee sighed. Her whole life was a sacrifice. Behind her Uncle George sighed too. He had hoped to sit next to her but had been balked in the aisle by Mrs. Phelum and found himself instead in a seat with the Old Lady. Even Uncle George had limits. He put a handkerchief over his face and settled down to fumble in his pockets and lose himself in rubbery dreams. The Old Lady, on the other hand, was determined not to miss a thing. She held Belinda up to the window and loudly articulated the name of everything they passed—hotel ... barbed wire ... dress maker's ... cemetery ... riot squad—until Belinda turned and bit her on the lip. Painful as it was to the Old Lady, the attack was a relief to the others who were no longer compelled obsessively to glance out of the window at every pronouncement but could get on with their own business.

Mrs. Phelum in a seat to herself settled down to read *My Pound-*

ing Heart. Behind her, Albert Hawkin was propounding his latest theory: that the universe was shaped like a giant egg timer that spiralled through nothingness while the galaxies slid about on its inside surface, negotiating the holes with which it was peppered by means of their own surface tension, in much the same way that the last drops of water in a colander will not go through, no matter how it is tipped. Haggerty, rendered insensible, had begun to snore.

At the back, Ben clutched his towel and swimming trunks and thought about getting there, while Gordon spat on his fingers and drew obscene pictures on the window. In the front seat, Scoria had begun to come round, uttering vicious testimonials on the Master's character and nudging Mildred every so often to ask "Inne?" or "Innit?" But Mildred held her face over a paper bag and could only moan.

It was an hour and a half's drive to Broadsands, for MacMillan. Jacky the Lackey, following in the Mercedes, was more than equal to the challenge but was hampered along the way by serious scruples concerning animate life, so that between obstacles he was forced to drive even faster.

Virginia Pinnacle sat very upright in stiff contemplation. Thirty minutes ago she had never been happier, with him beside her on the grey leather. A marriage could not have been more fulfilling. And then abruptly everything had changed and he was off. To send a fax from the house, he had said. Long distance. Leaving her queenly on the upholstery. And no sooner had he gone than *she* had appeared. Wafting down the front steps in her usual rag-bag of coloured scarves and drapery remnants, the latest infant at her shoulder. She looked like a balloon accident. No shoes either.

Virginia wished she had been able to think quickly enough. If she'd known he wasn't coming back she could have said, 'Drive on.' She had always wanted to use that phrase. But she had missed her moment. The woman had opened the door.

"Ah! He's not here yet."

"Mr. Pinnacle has gone into the house for a moment."

"Ah!" She had leaned in and deposited the damp baby on the crisp navy blue linen.

Virginia Pinnacle raised her head so as not to smell the milk. Cali settled herself beside her with much jangling of bangles, drawing her legs up to cross them on the seat. She reached over to take the baby.

"Babies!" she said. "Yummm!" and produced a breast. Virginia Pinnacle glared.

"Quite," she said. "They are such joy," her mouth turning down slightly as if she had just tasted something a little off.

Cali bent to nuzzle the sucking face. "Oh, sometimes," she said—she had hoped to perform for both of them, but this audience of one was almost as good—"sometimes I could just ..." She extended a very deep pink tongue and slid it across the child's eyelid. Virginia Pinnacle plumbed the depths of disgust.

It was at that moment that the car phone had twittered and Jacky had reached round to answer it.

"Yeah? Right, mate. No sweat." He put the phone back. "He ain't comin'," he said, getting in. "'Somethin's come up.' So, if you're ready, ladies, we're gonna get our asses outta here."

Cali hissed through her teeth. "He bit me," she lied with a smile, blaming the baby. Though it was she who had the urge to bite and more than just a nipple. The whole point of the exercise was lost. She felt as if she had been tricked.

But now the salt from the baby's eyelid was on her tongue and the sea was not to be denied. The child opened its eyes and smiled woozily; the milk ran out of the side of its mouth and down its neck. And so Cali licked it up and savoured it and at last settled back. Virginia Pinnacle resigned herself to an hour and a half of misery.

Tots sat with her eyes trained on the streets and houses ribboning by. They had left the grand, dilapidated mansions, left the abandoned tower blocks standing with their huge KEEP CLEAR signs around their necks like bottles of liquor dressed in vulgar labels, passed the parks where twelve-foot wire fences protected the yellow grass and the dust-laden trees, passed the machine works, which lay silent and the flour mill, which operated twice a year and was patrolled by dogs.

Now, making detours round the No-go zones when he had to, MacMillan raced past rows of identical shuttered houses through streets which were mostly empty except at food depots where long lines of the waiting hopeful wound round on themselves.

There was a big Outlet out on the edge of the downs in the buildings of an old air force base. It was accessible only to those who could still acquire fuel and a vehicle that worked. The parking lot displayed an assortment of mobile scrap belonging, presumably, to the patrons and several shiny administration vehicles. Perhaps in fond memory of the heyday of road accidents, the Government had refurbished a pub just down from the Outlet. It was fast approaching. Morgan got up and went to the front of the bus, bending to put her lips close to MacMillan's ear. Belinda slid from the Old Lady's lap and Gordon cracked his nose on the seat in front as MacMillan trod on the brakes. He thought it was the best idea yet but was above saying so and only signalled his approval by veering across the road to the Nag's Head, still braking, in front of the only other car they had seen on the road in ten minutes. The sound of the passing driver's horn diminished rapidly as if it were being sucked into the more distant reaches of the universe.

"Ladies toilets on the left. Gents on the right. Back at the coach in fifteen minutes." MacMillan pulled up abruptly at the front entrance with a tub of plastic marigolds under his front wheel.

His passengers climbed down shakily and made straight for the bar, except Mildred, who said she needed air, and the two boys, who wandered off disconsolately to the neglected beer garden. Tots was going to make her way to the Ladies but stopped when she saw the lorry with the logo on its side that belonged to the brewery not far from the House in Pimlico. There was a tarp in the back but nothing else. She ran to find Ben.

He was sitting patiently near a couple who had covered their hairless heads with scarves and sat holding hands and staring into their empty glasses. Gordon was looking for cigarette butts. Tots sat at the broken table and waited until Gordon was out of earshot.

She leaned across to Ben. "I'm going back," she whispered.

"You can't."

"I can."

"What for?"

"I might find them papers. Don't matter if I don't, though. I've made up me mind. I'm leavin' anyway."

"But you can't get back."

"I'm hitchin' a lift."

"You won't be able to get in."

"Haggerty's flap.'

Ben had to think fast or be condemned to a day with only Gordon for company. "Father will still be there."

"Course he won't. 'Out of town.' You know what that means?"

"No."

"He's flyin' off somewhere, inne? Like he always does. Sunnier climes. That's a joke. Anyhow he'll be long gone. Which is what I'll be in a little while. So say 'Bye'."

"All right," said Ben. 'Bye' would not come. 'Bye' stuck in his throat and made it hard to swallow.

"Only don't tell no one? No one, right?"

Gordon was calling.

"Promise?"

"Come on, Ben, you shithead!" Foul even from a distance.

"Promise?"

"I promise."

Ben ran off. When he reached Gordon he looked back but Tots had gone. There was only a brewer's lorry pulling out of the forecourt. Inside the Nag's Head everyone waited for the Old Lady, who had adhered faithfully to the role fate and the song had assigned her and managed to get stuck in the lavatory. Tottering in after two glasses of gin, which she shared with Belinda, she had failed to totter out again. A small crowd had gathered. The air had clogged with advice and directions—chief of which was "Pick up the bloody dog!" Belinda snarled and snapped. She darted forward from the cubicle like a Moray eel from its lair, lusting for chunks as hands and feet explored under the door. There were those who began to curse. Someone brought Haggerty a toilet roll to bind his thumb. Mildred said sagely, "Stitches." Haggerty said the top part would knit back on. No trouble.

"Two minutes," said MacMillan from the hallway where he leaned, smoking, and the babble increased, syllables colliding. But the Old Lady heard none of it—or so it was reasonable to assume, for she continued to say nothing at all.

"Out of the way, you lot," said Morgan. "Now gi'e me a leg up." The biddable Sherilee clasped her fingers and cupped her hands to receive the black shoe. MacMillan watched from behind his cigarette smoke. MacMillan who never lowered himself for anyone might have given away his wheels for that particular thrill.

"That's my girl," said Mrs. Phelum. "If I was a few pounds lighter." And were she less jaunty with rum.

Morgan hoisted her tight skirt to her hips and swung herself up and almost over the top of the door. But she did not succeed. Belinda was waiting. Fuelled perhaps by the gin, she sprang to within an inch of the dangling ankle. It may be that Morgan had finally succumbed to the effect of accumulated years of irritation in the service of the Old Lady; in any event she behaved quite unlike herself and it shamed her when she thought about it later at the picnic and knew that she would have abandoned the old woman forever, for "Sod that!" was her first and only reaction, whereupon she climbed down and returned to the bar.

She found Scoria there too. Scoria was sciving, or about to. Morgan diplomatically turned her back, though she had seen: a grey-haired biker, rings, studs. She remembered the beautiful black Kawasaki outside. More to offer than a plate of old hen on a cliff top. Well, not long now and they could all scive off, if only into oblivion. She knocked back Scoria's drink, too.

MacMillan looked at his watch.

"Board the bus." He shouldered himself off the door jamb where he had been leaning, ground his cigarette into the parquet and left.

The crowd at the Ladies looked at one another then at the door to the cubicle, apology implicit in their eyebrows. Not a scruple among them.

"I'll call the fire-brigade," said Uncle George, and squared his shoulders to emphasize that it was man's work.

"Never say die," said Mrs Phelum.

But there were noises now from inside and the bolt drew back. The Old Lady came out blinking.

"Such a lovely nap," she said.

In the Dark

U nder the tarpaulin in the back of the lorry, Tots had no way of knowing if she was indeed going to Pimlico. The driver had seemed to take the right turning out of the forecourt but from that moment Tots was fully occupied with an empty barrel that had not been secured. It was something of a disappointment after the discomfort and bruises to find herself not in Pimlico less than a quarter of a mile from the house as she had hoped, but in Battersea, which was considerably further. Her lorry driver it seemed had other business to attend to. From what she could make out as she carefully climbed down and sidled out of sight, he was doing a spot of graft for a mate.

She edged away out of sight and began to walk. With the approach of midday, the streets were all but deserted. It was too hot for walking. The remaining roots of the work ethic had shrivelled in the rising temperatures that followed the years of cold, and the surviving population had rediscovered the good sense of less cock-eyed cultures: if it was hot they stayed in the shade; if they were tired they slept.

The heat beat up from the paving stones, and the river, as Tots crossed the bridge, glittered. She had left the Day Out before she had caught even a whiff of the sea. And nothing could make Tots's blood run faster than the tang of salt on the lip and raunchy smell of kelp—except perhaps that tell-tale that precedes any other, that first glimpse, the electric spider's thread of light stretched along the horizon beyond the empty landscape. Nothing, not even the thing itself was as mysteriously thrilling as the intimation. And she was missing it. She wondered what she was doing going off by herself. She had to assure herself that it would all be worth it, that perhaps after today every day would be a Day Out. There might even be just Out. Just the silver sea.

She walked past a group of children and stopped to make sure she was still going in the right direction. Three of them, younger than herself, were employed in stamping on the fingers of a fourth who appeared to have fallen down the area in front of one of the big houses. He clung to the bottom of the railings, shouting protest and imprecation but not crying, while they gave her directions and continued to stamp.

"Thanks," she said. "Now leave off. Poor little bleeder."

One of them picked up a piece of rubble and threw it at her back. The others too looked for bits to throw. The child in the area took advantage of the distraction and scrambled up and out.

And now she could not imagine why the indentures had assumed such importance for her. She was going back, yes, to find the other half. There was the question of protecting herself; that was still important. Leaving the Master with her indentures still in his possession meant leaving him still with a hold over her; they were strings of a net he could, would pull tight. He could get any number of strays to replace her—but he wouldn't. Possession engendered jealousy; he would have to get her back. So that was part of it, but not all. She had thought she needed to find the indentures just to hold them whole, both halves, in her hands, this evidence of self of herself. She had imagined how she would give it to Ben. He would look at it under his long lashes and his mouth would pronounce her name—and she would become somehow whole, somehow more than she already was. Now she was not so sure that it mattered any more, to find that missing half. It wouldn't really matter if it was blank. A new instinct told her that everything she would be she already was. Nothing the Master had cooked up would give her anything more. If she needed anything she needed the spider's thread of light, out there, at the horizon.

But she was nevertheless almost at the door and had no alternative but to carry on. In case Ben was right and the Master should still be at home, Tots took care to be quiet approaching the House. She went round the back to the scullery door. The makeshift cat-flap that Hagggerty had installed for Roger's nightly excursions was, as Mrs. Phelum had put it, seriously big, and to make matters worse had been installed back to front, letting the cat in but not out. Mrs. Phelum wouldn't have minded having it boarded up. Tots bent down and turned her head sideways to ease herself in. She got one arm through and rested her hands on the floor while she wriggled to free her other shoulder.

"Look what's dragging itself in, then!"

The flap bounced hard on Tots's head as, instinctively, she flinched.

"Gawd, it's you!" It was the only time in her life she had been pleased, or anyway relieved, to see Scoria. "You didn't half give me a fright."

"Oh, yeah?" said Scoria, stuffing forks into her shoulder bag. "Don't gimme that crap. You're a plant." A puzzling statement, Tots thought, until she realized they were back in Chicago. "How long you been tailin' me?"

"I haven't."

"Yeah, like hell, you haven't." Scoria closed the bulging bag with difficulty. *"Oh, Scoria,"* she simpered, *"fancy seeing you here! What-a-pleasant-surprise-who-would-have-thought-it?"*

Tots, experienced in staying out of range of Scoria's venom, kept quiet. The maid picked up one of the two heavy suitcases beside her. "Wanna look?" she demanded.

"No, but I'll give you a hand."

Scoria raised an eyebrow. "Thanks. You'd be about as handy as a limp dick with this lot."

Tots, possessor of amazing wiry strength of limb as well as mind, picked up the other suitcase.

"I suppose you'd like to see it *acks*idently fall open, an' all?"

"Oh, get on," said Tots. "I don't want to know what's in your old suitcase."

Heading through the kitchen and up the stairs to the front hall, Scoria stopped. A new thought bubbled up to the miry surface of her mind.

"What you really come back for?" she asked.

"Somethin' I left behind."

"Oh, yeah? What?"

"Me papers." Tots sighed. "My contrack."

Now Scoria was unsure. "Nah," she said. "You've come back to knock off somethin' for yourself. You was going to do a job of your own, wasn't you?" She could not help but admire. One so young. "Why dontcha get what you want an' come with us?"

"Who's us?"

"Me an' my new boyfriend. From the pub. Didn't you see him outside? On his bike."

Tots did not think so.

"Well, he'll be back in a mo'. He said he had somethin' else to pick up—apart from me. Wanna come?"

"No thanks," said Tots. "I think I'll stay an' look for me papers. You got yours?"

"Don't need none. Write me own."

Tots was ready to hear more of this startling new concept, but they had reached the front door. Which would not open.

"How d'you get out this bleedin' place?"

"Up there." Tots pointed to the hook where a key for the burglar lock hung.

"Right," said Scoria, unlocking. "That'll come in handy," and she slipped the key in her pocket. "Oh, hang on." She drew out a tangle of silver chains charms and selected a thin disc, the surface of which had been engraved over a pattern of irregular lines. She handed it to Tots. This is yours. See? 'Tots.' Yours to keep an' treasure." She laughed. "Ta-ra."

Tots watched as she took the other suitcase and went down the steps, groggy with the weight. There was no Kawasaki. There was no boyfriend.

"What will you do, now?" Though it was risking a scourging.

Scoria turned round. Her face was wiped clean of malice. "Oh, I'll find some old bastard to work for—an' I'll screw him rigid, that's what I'll do."

"Oh." What could you say to that? "Good luck."

Tots closed the door and stood looking at the silver disc—which was most certainly not silver—and her name and something else engraved there. Perhaps this was what she had come back for. She heard Scoria's footsteps coming back up to the door. The dead bolt clunked a few times. "Just checking." Scoria laughed. "Never know when I might want to 'slip back' for somethin', eh?"

Down by the Sea

A s if he had been waiting all his life for just such an innocent, unsuspecting victim to approach, MacMillan shot out of the parking lot across the path of the oncoming Fiat with murderous panache and made good, not to say astonishing, time down the deserted motorway. The speed did not do Mildred any good. She had run out of bags and was negotiating for more. Cali was the only one to catch the first glimpse of Broadsands glittering in the midday sun. Cali had joined the coach at the Nag's Head. Virginia Pinnacle had been clever, waiting until Cali got out of the car. "No," she had said. "I've changed my mind. I shan't have a drink after all. Drive on, Jacky." *Drive on*. It was one of those milestones in a person's life. Not everybody reached it. Just a shame it had to be Jacky when she said it; he looked good, but 'MacMillan' sounded so much better.

Cali focused on the distant light. She could not wait. Mrs. Phelum beside her thought she heard her growl, though it could have been hunger.

The bus plunged on through the town, scorched along beside the promenade, and ground uphill again to the cliff-top. Cali was already standing up. The smell of the sea, even with its overtones of toxic waste had invaded every byway of her body, sluiced her senses and woken every cell Quickly she knotted a large cotton square across her shoulder and plumped the baby into it, then she sashayed hip-first happily down the aisle past the rest of them still scrabbling in bags and reaching under seats.

MacMillan stared in contempt as she swung down the steps. "Bloody hippy," he muttered.

Once down, she began to run on bare brown feet across the grass to the edge, to the very brink of the cliff, where she stood with her face to the light while the wind dug its fingers into her scalp and pillowed her buttocks under her lifting skirt.

And the sea danced. All decked in spangles it danced, perfect partner to her exhilaration.

She reached into the sling for the infant, drew it out and swung it high above in one smooth motion so that MacMillan, the only one who saw, thought, *Here she goes*, believing her ready indeed to hurl the child high, to make of it an acrobatic gull, and said "Christ!" as it left her hands. It put out its arms and legs. Never had MacMillan looked so hard; as she caught it and drew it back to her, its shape remained imprinted on his retina: starfish against the blue, a missing piece of sky.

She placed it square on her shoulders and its fingers clutched her hair while it blinked amazed against the brightness it had seen. MacMillan was disappointed. He turned his attention to the bus, opening up the baggage locker and bumping the hampers out to the accompaniment of chipping china and tinkling glass.

"You mind them!" said Mrs. Phelum, her heart and soul manhandled. It was distressing. Uncle George lit a fresh cigar and summoned Haggerty who came, rumpled and dog-eared, to lend a massive hand. Together they bore the hampers out to the open green, where Morgan and Sherilee put down their shoulder bags and spread out the blue and white cloth. A cliff-top target for sky-divers. Morgan would have liked a paratrooper to drop in right then. Sherilee wondered whether Mrs. Phelum had remembered to pack the custards.

"Sorry!" Uncle George's behind nudged hers as he set down another basket. "Good Lord! Excuse me!" As if he never would have dreamed.

"Creep!" said Morgan, keeping the word between her teeth. Sherilee giggled.

Uncle George kept the giggle in mind for later. "Now where's Haggerty? Ah, Haggerty. Be a good chap will you and open some of this plonk while I see where Mrs. Pinnacle has got—" But he did not have to bother. The Mercedes was just drawing up next to the bus.

It stopped and Jacky, beaming, opened the door for Virginia. His blood still purred with the beauty of the car, which he had taken on not a few detours, just to savour its performance.

"Uncle George!" The glassy voice froze more than marrow; no one moved. Virginia Pinnacle stood making an impatient little gesture with her gloves, slapping them into her palm as if trying to bring new life to a pair of kippers. Fine figure of a woman, George had always thought. The first one wasn't a patch on her. A brick, too, having to put up with having Wife Number One under the same roof. You had to hand it to Ralph.

"You best get over there and see what she wants," said Mrs. Phelum.

George left, fantasies springing quick as toadstools at every step.

"I do not see a scrap of shade. Of any kind."

"Oh?" He looked along the bare greensward; it was striped grey and green where the wind had combed the dust back towards the town. He tapped his foot for inspiration.

"None," continued Virginia. "How do you suppose we're going to feel after an afternoon of this?"

"There is a tree." Though even he would have to admit, if forced, that it was distant and did not possess much leaf.

MacMillan, his hands deep in his pockets had wandered closer. Here was entertainment. He watched their faces in turn. Ping. Pong. Ping. She never missed a shot.

Uncle George used his shoulders to rake in a gigantic breath while he drew up his eyebrows. Virginia persisted.

"What are you going to do?"

The eyebrows climbed higher. His shoulders were at his ears.

"Oh, you ...." Now more than ever Virginia Pirstine longed to be a bona fide Pinnacle and call him a stupid man without repercussions.

"'Scuse me," Jacky the Lackey had been waiting for his moment. If he played his cards right, he might find himself with a new job, permanently, funny uniform and all. The car was the sexiest thing he'd had his hands on in a long time. "'Scuse me," he said. "Shall I have lunch brought over?" He was pleased with the phrase that had sprung out of nowhere; it stood more chance of success than "What if I bring you a bite in the car?"

"Yes. Please. Thank goodness someone has some sense." Virginia glowered at George. Who only shrugged.

Not with a barge pole, he thought and was glad that his fantasies had never seen the light of day. *Not with a barge pole.*

Ben and Gordon on the zig-zag path down to the promenade looked like pebbles in a chute. They skittered out at the kiosk at the bottom that had once sold buckets and spades and inflatable beach toys. There was nothing to buy now, but on its painted shutters the fat ladies in polka-dot bikinis still expostulated while their skinny shamefaced men leered. Gordon stayed to ogle and ponder.

On either side of the kiosk a line of deck chairs extended along the promenade, their sagging green canvas collecting dust and sand until the next strong wind ballooned it out again. For the benefit of the convalescents and the old who sheltered under their black umbrellas from the dangerous rays, municipal loudspeakers relayed the same recording over and over: voices that took to the wind and sparred with gulls, tinny voices of children who pitted themselves against the booming sea, and drowned laughing. In the deckchairs the old people listened and remembered, or slept, dreaming, and forgot.

The dry sand above the high-water mark was still open though the area below had been closed for years, cut off from the rest by a wire fence strung between the breakwaters. To reduce their liability still further, the town council had hung notices like dirty washing on the fence: *WARNING: DO NOT PASS BEYOND THIS POINT*, *WARNING: SWIMMING IN THE OCEAN HAS BEEN ASSOCIATED WITH SERIOUS MUTAGENIC DISEASE AND DEATH.*

Ben ducked under the first one. The wind, coming off the sea, picked up the splintered cries and shouts of the recording and carried them back towards the cliffs. On this side of the fence there was only the vastness of the sea itself upon the eardrum, a presence felt rather than heard at this distance, for the tide was far out and the noise of the waves was indistinguishable from the soft boom of the wind. Other trespassers wandered there on the wet sand among the half-submerged engine blocks and old TVs. They stepped silently through the deltas of polystyrene particles left by the draining tide, marginals all, all isolates, stepping in and out of each other's field of vision.

The tide was further out than Ben had thought. The sea was sliding over the edge. He began to run, the ridges of sand hard and unfamiliar against the soles of his feet. A small bubble of anxiety began to rise in his lungs and broke only when he reached the reaching edge of the sea and found the ancient conundrum of water changing unchanged.

The small surf receding fizzed between his toes. He saw Cali too further along standing at the edge and he went to stand beside her.

"It's warm."

"I knew it would be."

"It's the best place."

"It's the only place. If one is to be anywhere."

They stood side by side and looked out across the unimaginable light, possessing. The dust that fell into it every day sank and began its pernicious permutations in the dark. Still it could only dazzle.

"It's supposed to be dirty."

"Oh, 'dirty'." Her voice was rimmed with scorn. "Of course it's dirty. It's contaminated. But that won't last. We will all be poisoned with it, but we shall die sooner than it and then it will recover. That is the beauty. We can destroy ourselves but there is no destroying it. It is the source."

Without moving his head, Ben slid his sceptical eyeballs to the extreme right of their sockets where they could watch her, if not comfortably, then without risk of discovery. She was clutching her baby to her, her arms crossed over its back, its face pressed between her breasts. Small movements suggested that it might be struggling to come up for air.

"Does baby like it?"

Cali heaved a great sigh, coming back from the deep.

"The sea? Oh, baby *belongs* to the sea." And she was hoisting her skirts with one hand, looping them into the leather belt around her hips and squatting to unwrap the baby and baptize it in the scummy foam.

Ben wished he had left well alone. And yet the baby looked happy.

"Babies are nice," he said. "You like babies, don't you?"

"I like babies, yes," her face strung like a kite above the baby's smile.

"Is this your last one?" Ben's innocence would have cleansed oceans.

"When I have my last child," Cali said softly, "I shall have no more purpose." She looked at Ben. He felt as if the centres of his pupils had opened; she was pouring in. "Mrs. Pinnacle will reign supreme."

"What will you do then?"

"What shall I have to do?"

"Where will you go?"

"Where shall I have to go?"

Ben got the feeling that Cali wasn't participating fully in this conversation any longer.

"Well. I'm going up for some food," he said.

Without looking up from the gurgling baby that she cradled in one arm, Cali hooked the other arm out and round his legs. "And if we stop the fathers," she said, and lay her cheek for a moment against his arm, "who shall stop the sons?"

This sounded like part of a conversation they hadn't had yet. Ben wormed free. "Bye," he called. Running. Just in case.

On the cliff top the considerable remains of lunch lay about on the blue and white cloth. Everything had been scooped, or sliced, broken or crumbled at least once; nothing had been finished. Mrs. Phelum's folding chair threatened to live up to its name beneath her. Mrs. Phelum, reluctant to disturb its delicate equilibrium, pretended not to notice. She would have liked a stove to put her feet on. And if only the recording of the bloody seagulls would shut up ....

"Bloody seagulls," muttered Morgan. She was slipping into the state she most enjoyed.

Sherilee said, "Horrid birds," and was wrong again.

"The'er marvellous birds," Morgan said. "Marvellous. They just make a noise, that's all. When all we want is a wee bit of peace."

Sherilee was glum, though not for long. Uncle George, the many-fingered molester, had taken stock, and decided that the time was ripe.

"Pecker up there." It was a problem for George, the opening gambit. Always had been. He liked as a rule to err on the side of inanity; it helped promote the innocent intention, mask the dastardly design.

Sherilee brightened at once. "Oh, it's you."

"You know, I believe it is. Ha-ha. Gained a pound or two in the last half hour or so but still the same old me," the waistcoat solid under the stiffly patting palm, "and raring to go."

Morgan could not bear any more. She got up, brushed the dust and bits of dry grass from her skirt, and made off towards one of the cliff paths, only a little crookedly, humming as she went. *We-know-what-you're-after*.

"Oh," said Sherilee, so bereft of willpower, so utterly limp and wilting and lack-a-day that she would surely at last be taken by the jolly George. Whose lucky day? "Where?"

"Where'er the winds of fate take us, m'dear."

"Oh." It could have been his arm, extended for her to lean on, this invitation. But it was not. Old George knew a thing or two. No spotting George in the act.

So they left, together, apart. To a sandy encounter behind a striped canvas erection that would flap like their hearts at the touch of the wind. Only Gordon saw them go and sensing something secret and forbidden followed at a distance. It could, he felt, have something to do with the fat lady in the polka-dot bikini.

In the Mercedes, Virginia Pinnacle had finished her lunch. The windows were down but the seats were sticky and the air was like a hot towel on her face, her face which she could not afford to lose. She didn't know where she would ever find another pot of Silken Sheen. She put her head back and tried to think cool thoughts: silver, marble, damask, mirrors, Meissen, ice, crystal; but they all made her think of dinner parties, even viscose, which is what she liked to wear to entertain, and it only made her hotter.

Haggerty lay on his back beside the sinking cook. He had covered his face with a tea-towel depicting the Tower of London.

"Hallo," said Ben, arriving hot and tired from the beach. "Where is everyone?"

He could see MacMillan and Jacky over at the bus, where MacMillan had the side of the hood up to display the hot oily innards.

Mrs. Phelum sighed, and considered. Mr. Hawkin, she knew, had gone for a walk with the Old Lady to the clock tower but she did not have the energy to construct the sentence. She opened her eyes and closed them again. "Morgan's over there," she managed before she went under a second time. She raised one hand vaguely in the direction of the edge of the cliff.

Ben looked and wondered for a moment if he had missed a moment of high melodrama and then he remembered there was a path. It was a small track cut into the face of the cliff and punctuated at intervals by natural recesses in which the Council had obligingly installed wooden benches. It was on one of these that Morgan sat very upright, describing slow circles with her upper torso as she blinked at the sea and sometimes belched.

"Hallo, Ben," she said, hearing his halting step.

"Hi. Where is everybody?"

"Where indeed?"

Ben was afraid she might want to continue where Cali had left off. He changed tack.

"It's a shame Father's not here."

"A terrible shame."

"Where do you suppose he is?"

"I should say he's either half-way to Tunisia on the Government jet or else he's standing on Vauxhall bridge waiting for the fireworks." She looked at her watch. "Or he will be in about an hour."

"Are you drunk?"

"Drunk but not disorderly. Or disreputable. Only down. Down at heart."

"Down in the dumps."

"Oh, in the dumps, yes. In the doldrums, in a deep depression, speaking de profundis—och, you wouldn't know about that. Down, down, down."

"Why?"

"I'm always down when I'm drunk. I love it. And today especially. I'm down for the count."

"Down for the count?"

"You know what I mean, Ben. Ten, nine, eight, seven, six ..."

"Blast off." Though he did not have a specific explosion in mind.

"Exactly." But Morgan did. She reached under the bench for a bottle and took a drink. "My biggest job and I'm not even there tae see it. Beautiful it will be. The flowering of my talent. A blooming, a cumulus, a culmination of my energy and expertise."

How adults loved to laud their own achievements. Ben had heard others do the same. He stood up. "Hey Gordon!" He could see his brother half-way down the cliff, crawling on all fours between gorse bushes.

Morgan, seeing her audience was about to desert her, caught him by the wrist. "Listen," she hissed. "Can you keep a secret?"

"Of course. I never tell. It's bad luck."

"Swear?"

"I swear."

"Your father and I ..."

"Yes?"

"... are in collusion."

Ben wondered if that made her his step-mother. He decided not to say much until she revealed a bit more.

"We are in cahoots, he and I. I am his accomplice and he is mine in a crime most heinous. And all for the piddly insurance."

"I don't understand."

"Your father and I are locked forever in our common guilt. From this day he has a hold over me as I have over him. Our fates are joined."

"Never mind," said Ben. It was all a bit heavy for a picnic and he was not quite sure what she meant. Joined with his father? He could see why she might be feeling down. He cast about for a consoling word. "I don't suppose anyone'll notice."

But Morgan reacted violently. "Breathe a word of this and I'm dead."

"I don't think you should have told me," said Ben. Her long fingers a handcuff on his wrist. "I really didn't want to know. It probably isn't any of my business."

"Oh, but it is. When you get back and you see what's left, you'll see that it is. But there was nae a thing I could do."

Now Ben began to feel uncomfortable. An ugly inkling grew. Was monstrous.

"The House, you see .... How can I put this wi'out upsetting you? The House—"

The truth exploded like the Fifth of November as she spoke. "—is going tae blow."

Stunned for a few seconds by the aftershock, Ben could only stare, unseeing. Then, "No!" he said. "Tots!"

"What do you mean 'Tots'?" The child, the silly, bloody little idiot, hadn't she seen her at the pub? Since the pub?

"She's in the house! Tots is in the House!"

"Don't gi'e me that bullshit, Ben. You're joking."

But Ben was screwing the top of the whisky bottle back on and stuffing it in her handbag. "Come on! Help me," he said.

"Help you what?"

"Get back. We have to get her out of there."

"All right, all right. Don't panic. There's lots of time, lots. We'll find a phone that's working." But as she stood up, Morgan's feet found themselves planted on two individually revolving, randomly tipping invisible plates and she rephrased her solution.

"You find a phone," she said and rifled in her purse for some change.

With his strange, hurdler's gait, Ben raced across the top of the cliff and down the zig-zag path to the pay phone at the kiosk. The phone itself was there inside the perspex bubble; but there was no receiver.

On his way back up, panting, his aching legs moving as if they were knee-deep in sand, it occurred to Ben that Tots would not answer the phone even if they could eventually find one that would make it ring.

The same thought had evidently occurred to Morgan, with a tonic effect on her faculties; she was over by the bus, against which the surly MacMillan leaned again. Jacky had gone to look for his friends the poets under the pier.

Morgan-The-Not-Very-Fey saw Ben coming, straggle-legged and out of breath, back up the path; leaning back so that MacMillan would not see, she shook her head. Ben slowed down and in doing so missed his first taste of X-rated suggestion. Not that Morgan said anything unbecoming, but she was sultry, not far from sizzling.

Leaning on the hood of the bus, the curve of her waist following its line, her shoulders back so that she met MacMillan's gaze breast on, she said something banal: "You don't like picnics, do you?" or, "Isn't it hot?" Whatever it was it had the effect of a poleaxe behind MacMillan's knees. She remarked that there were too many people; there was no one on the cliff walk. She dropped the information like a pair of silk drawers.

MacMillan's eyes left her breast. Her long fingers were unfastening the clasp of her handbag. It might have been her clothing. She managed to open the bag just long enough to reveal the presence of the amber Scotch inside. She wetted her lips and lifted her eyelids lazily, her eyelashes the fringes of a tawdry curtain that rose on scenes of outrageous indiscretion and exquisite excess.

"You should try it,"she said. "I might come by, myself, in a wee while." And he felt as if her hands were already in his pants, which indeed one of them was—or in his pocket at least—though it was after rewards less carnal and more practical by far.

"Quick," she said to Ben as MacMillan strolled away towards the cliff edge, twitching and tugging at his clothes as if he could hardly keep them from flying off him. "Quick, get in! And keep down."

She swung up the steps behind him and into the driver's seat.

"Where's the bloody keyhole?" In all her jobs her voice had never been so urgent.

Obligingly, Ben pointed it out and the bus, growling for the handbrake to be released, bucked once and shot towards a row of litter drums.

"Oh. Where's he off to, then?" said Mrs. Phelum with vast indifference. And Morgan's driving, after the best part of the bottle, was indeed on a par with the chauffeur's.

MacMillan himself, his ears ringing from his rocketing blood, did not even turn round. Trickily missing the drums, Morgan sped away, blinking hard to sober up. Every time she blinked, she noticed, the scene ahead had changed. It was like viewing slides through her windshield, each blink was a click that moved the picture on. How she got from one scene to the next was a profound mystery—but she did, and in one piece. In the space of fifty clicks they were careening round the cloverleaf out of the town.

Morgan began to feel better. "Don't you worry about a thing, laddie," she said. "We're going tae make it. Lots of time, lots. You'll see." She looked at her watch and put her foot down harder.

The road ahead was clear and with Morgan's head clearing, too, they did indeed make good time. Morgan, for no apparent reason, began to laugh and shake her head.

"What's wrong?" asked Ben.

"Och, nothing's wrong. I was just thinking. All for one wee lassie. Wi'out even a name tae call her own."

"That's what she went back for."

Morgan looked at Ben.

"And she wants to run away."

"There's a lot of people run away because they know who they are."

"Doesn't everybody know—apart from Tots, I mean?"

"I guess not. Everybody ought tae know. You'd think it'd be the first thing they'd know. The only thing."

"But someone has to tell them." For Ben this was illumination.

"Exactly. Then they have tae decide."

"What?"

"Whether tae believe what they're told."

"It will be awful if you've killed her."

Morgan squeezed her eyes shut suddenly as if she had heartburn. "Thank you, Ben," she said. "Thanks a lot."

She had begun to feel a little sick, although she had eaten nothing all day. She looked at her watch again. "No. She's all right for a while longer. She may not even be there. The little beggar."

"You like her don't you?"

"Me? Och, yes. I like her fine. Why don't we change the subject. Have you ever been this fast before? I wonder what your Gordon would say if he could see us now."

"I know what Tots would say. She'd say, 'You better watch it, you had. You'll get done'."

As they passed the Nag's Head they came upon a patrol car and an ancient tow truck at the scene of an accident which seemed to involve only one vehicle, an overturned Fiat. Morgan swung out and passed without losing speed.

"They waved to us," said Ben. And when Morgan looked in her mirror she saw that men—police—were indeed waving, waving and pointing in her direction and gesturing. About time she thought, if she were to be honest with herself.

"Oh, God," she said and blew a hole in the exhaust as she changed down.

Sober now, she burned through the suburbs like a Formula One driver. She was in Le Mans. While her brain coolly processed all the moving furniture of the world, her hands and feet, in faultless conversation with the engine, coaxed it to fresh feats of astonishing verve. With a salvo of changing gears they crossed the river and headed towards Pimlico. All would have been well had Morgan not decided to try a few short cuts.

The bus squealed into and out of back streets, side streets, even a mews, only to come unstuck, or more accurately, stuck, in an alleyway two blocks from the house. Jammed fast between the jutting sills of bricked up windows, the bus would not move. Neither forward nor back nor any way to the side would it move and Morgan and Ben knew they were finished. They looked at each other with raised eyebrows, their ears still ringing from the wrenching metal. Morgan brought her teeth together on an oath, which thrashed there for a moment and gave up.

"We'll have tae make a run for it," she said and pulled a lever. The door gasped once with the sound of someone receiving a blow in the diaphragm. But there was no way out: the bricks of the building to that side, complete with their wide streak of borrowed paint from the bus, formed a second, impenetrable wall.

Morgan looked at her watch and said "Shit!"

"What? What's the time?"

"Nothing, no time. Plenty of time. Look, if we can get you out of this bloody bus, you can still make it."

"The back!"

Ben scrambled to the back of the bus and threw himself at the emergency lever. The window, hinged at the top, ground open slowly, leaving a gap along its bottom edge of about nine inches.

"There! That's enough for a squirt like you. Now get out, quick!" Morgan pushed him like wet washing through a mangle and he half tumbled, half slid down the back of the bus.

"Run like bloody hell!" she shouted as he picked himself up. "You've got six minutes. If you don't make it in four, don't go in—" his hopeful soles were snatching him away, "—just keep the hell out of it. It's going tae go sky high. Start counting!"

He would stay away. Wouldn't he? Oh, wouldn't he? She watched his uneven, stumbling run. She'd committed a lot of criminal acts in her time but she'd never harmed a soul. Let alone two.

She decided it was time to get herself out of this ridiculous position and she worked at the window until she had forced it up a little higher. Carefully she positioned herself along the top of the back seat, ready to roll out under the window. But it was too late, she could hear the sirens and, staring at the end of the alleyway, she knew what she would shortly see.

She waited for the patrol car to cruise down and stop behind the bus. It would be so much more convenient to step down onto the hood, especially in such a tight skirt.

The Sound of Music

As soon as she closed the door on Scoria, Tots was overtaken by a sense of dereliction and a great loneliness. It was as if she stood inside a giant snail shell, chamber upon empty chamber spiralling above her. Even so, when she reached the great carved doors of the nursery she knocked. The House creaked once and a smatter of plaster fell to the floor somewhere in an upper room.

"Now or never," she said to herself and went in. The light did not work. She went over to the window and drew back the velvet curtains. Quills of brilliance waved in the thick green light.

Dust motes danced. Outside, the iron railings of the balcony disappeared in the dusty leaf. Where a python would not have lounged amiss.

Tots turned to survey the room. In the centre, where she remembered an enticement of cushion and down was a rat's nest of dusty rag. It looked as if it might do with a good shake out. Even in this light, Tots could see that the hangings on the wall were threadbare. She did not remember this lurid, underwater gloom. It was lugubrious; the room had drowned in its own stillness. Only the wands of light mocked. She walked through to the shrine. The alcove was nothing more than a place in the wall where the bricks had fallen away. She had thought the figure was squatting; it seemed now that it might be dancing—a curious low-slung movement to be sure, but there was something mobile in the tilt of the pelvis, the placement of the feet. The feet. Now Tots knew where Scoria had found the medallion: the statue had been ankle deep in silver, its feet plunged in a tangle of coins and charms. They were all gone.

She felt in her pocket and took out the medal. Two trees on either side of a pond. A snake beside one of the trees. For once Scoria had not lied. And there was more, but the marks were as haphazard for Tots as sparrows' feet in the dust. A shame it wasn't silver. She closed her fist. With the shock of a crateful of empties dropped on the pavement, she recognized it. A milk bottle top. The thing was made from two milk bottle tops pressed together over a disc. The foil was pressed flat, ironed to a one-dimensional smoothness and wrapped over the disc, maybe a dog tag. A bingo token.

As she stared at it, a door opened and closed in her mind. Opened: bang. And shut: bang. Opened. *Morning!* Bang. Opened and shut. Opened and shut. *Morning!* Bang. *Morning!* Coming out of Cali's door. *Morning!* Bang. *Morning! Just getting the empties!* But Cali didn't have any empties, was her own one-woman dairy, for God's sake. And Mrs. Phelum didn't need any; she had Lilly. *Morning!* Not once but often. The same two feet of film played over and over. Bang! The cat-flap slammed on the kitchen door downstairs and Tots jumped.

Someone had come in.

She held her breath, kept perfectly still, listening. Someone was running. She heard feet on the stairs coming up, knew at once the familiar syncopated gait before she heard the voice.

"Tots! Tots!" It was not far from a scream.

She went out to the hall muttering.

"Talk about givin' anyone a fright—"

"Tots!"

"Keep your hair on! I'm up here."

"Oh, Tots—" Ben appeared from the back stairs, out of breath, his mouth an ugly rectangle sucking air, "Oh, Tots—" He put out his hand. The words clogged his throat. They would not come out.

"Never knew you cared."

He shook his head. His mouth a gaping tunnel, wordless.

"You should have said."

"Come on!" he managed at last and his mouth took on a shape she had seen only once before, on the face of a woman in a photograph from an old war. She let herself be pulled towards the door and Ben lunged for the handle.

"Tots!" He was all to pieces, shrieking now. "Tots!"

"Here, get out the way." Tots tried the door. "It's that bloody burglar lock," she said. "You need the key."

Ben turned round, blind, desperate. "Oh, we're going to die! Together!"

Tots stared.

"We're going to blow up!"

"What?" But she knew, she did not need to know more, except perhaps why she had not caught the scent of it sooner. The smell of danger was all about the boy, his hair, his clothes, he reeked with it.

"In about forty-five seconds."

"No bloody way, we're not. Come on!" She grabbed his arm and tore back and up the main staircase, skinning shins, to the ballroom. The piano faced the door.

"Get up on there, quick!" She shoved him up so that he knelt on the keyboard, his upper body bent over the top of the piano. Darting round to the other end, she kicked the wedge out from under the wheel. At once the great piano began to roll, minim by minim, forward, gaining tempo. Tots turned and raced back towards the door. Ben, appalled craned for her.

"Tots!"

"Stay low!" she yelled, spinning now and running back again, hitting the piano at the moment it picked up speed, adding just enough momentum to send it trundling, unstoppable, the two of them on top, to the window, through the window and out, taking the frame, the wall, like a great ship launched with a shower of broken glass and bricks and a jangle of strings out over the harbour of the garden. Its black bulk cleared the courtyard and clipped off the mermaid's head, opening its lid to spring, fling Tots and Ben from it, flies from a swatter, before plunging to demolish itself in a deafening cataclysm of sound and crumple under a final brilliant cadenza on the garden path.

Ben got up slowly from the patch of dead-nettles where they had landed.

"Chykoffsky would have liked that," said Tots.

But Ben did not hear. His face grave and amazed, his self wholly centred in a truth both profound and obvious, he was transfigured by knowledge.

"We're alive," he said.

Tots did not have time to answer for at that moment the Taiwanese alarm clock inside the detonator under the main staircase made a small click as a metal plate on the flywheel struck a pin which slipped from its socket and released a spring and set in motion the chain of tiny events that blew the top off the House.

Ben and Tots covered their heads against the avalanche of debris as pieces of chimney breast and lead piping fell from the sky through the turmoil of liberated dust. Floorboards and chair legs and bits of dressing table followed. Tots saw none of it, her eyes were fixed on the roiling clouds of glory, billowing molten gold, through which numerous heavenly *putti* descended laughing and kicking their heels.

When she looked again, the rain had thinned to teaspoons and floppy disks. The door of the coal-house was open and Lilly was already eating the grey weeds.

Seeing a house where they had expected none was almost a disappointment, but it was there, its untrue walls unbelievably standing, however shakily, black smoke billowing where the roof should have been and, behind its blown windows, the red light of the fire pulsing. Tots turned to Ben. Shocked into imbecility, she was staring now with her teeth over her lower lip. He got up on his knees and nudged her hard.

She began to cry, suddenly and noisily. "Sorry," he said. "I didn't mean to upset you."

Tots shook her head. "No. It's not you. It's me papers. I'll never find them now. They're gone. Forever!" Her hooing was loud enough to muffle consolation. Ben had to shout.

"But Tots, they don't matter. Not any more. Oh, Tots, listen.

Can't you hear me? They don't matter."

She sniffed, suspicious.

"Your papers don't matter. Everything will be burned. Father's papers too. Everything."

In the ravaged landscape of Tots's prospects the smoke began to clear.

"There was a fire," she said, rehearsing. "And I disappeared. Right?"

"Right."

"Just like that."

"Just like that."

Now she was all wet teeth, tears.

"Funny. I spent all that time lookin'. Anyhow I got this. Look. You can read it to me." She took the medallion out of her pocket and waited. Ben read.

"'*To Tots. From Your Loving Father.*' So who is he?"

"Who do you think? Milk-o!"

Ben stumbled over his recently acquired notions of conception and birth.

"Left on the doorstep next to the milk?"

"Well, that's not quite what I meant, no. But if you want to put it like that. Comes to the same thing. Even when you know, it don't make no difference. She never cared about me one way or the other—nor about you," she added in case he should feel superior. "But I shouldn't let it worry you. You can waste a lot of time worryin'. Best thing is to get on with it. Like we just did."

Ben thought he might have been acknowledged for making this very observation himself just the other day in the coal-shed when she had decided they were related, but he chose to keep quiet.

"Now," she continued, "are you coming or not?"

"Me?"

"Why not?"

"You're the one who wants to run away."

The roar from inside the house was steady now, the glow almost cheerful. "You mean you want to stay?"

"This is my house."

"Was."

"But you can go. You can go whenever you want. I'll wait here till they come back. I won't tell Father."

"He's not coming back, your father. When did you last see him?

You'll never see him. He's not going to show up now."

"Well, Mother, then."

"Mrs. Pinnacle?"

"Yes."

"You serious?"

Ben was silent. The ashes of his parents were snowing on him, dusting his hair.

"Tots?"

"What?"

"I'm afraid."

"I'm the one supposed to be afraid—and I am. But that don't change nothin'. Now are you comin' or not?"

"Where are you going?"

"Lord love a duck. How do I know?"

"I just thought there might be somewhere ..."

"I expect there is. It's just findin' it, innit?"

Ben seemed satisfied with this logic, but then he turned away.

"You go and look," he said, "and I'll wait here. Until I'm ready."

It was the final confirmation, as if she had needed more, of what she had known all along. She saw the first of the looters picking through the fall-out. The body of the mermaid lay on its back under a sprinkling of the fine warm snow. She could hear sirens.

"See you, then," she said and brushed herself down. "And thanks, Ben. For comin' back."

She began to walk away, stepping over rubble as she went. She thought he might call after her. Her ears drummed with wanting to hear.

About the Author

Pauline Holdstock was born in England and graduated from London University in English, French and History. She has taught in England, the Bahamas and Canada. Her short fiction pieces have been published in several Canadian literary magazines. She now lives on Vancouver Island.

Photo: John Holdstock